I0589087

Bittersweet Short Stories

Ten Tales of Life, Love and Mortality

by

Linda Robson Bell

Dedication

To my family.......no need to say any more

Robson Ryder Publishing
Suite 96/78 William Street
East Sydney NSW 2011

ISBN 978-0-646-95057-0

Short stories--fiction

Stories

Acknowledgements

Thank you to my daughter Emma for reading and editing this manuscript, offering wise and thoughtful feedback and unwavering support. Thank you to my husband Robert for all his support, patience and encouragement of my writing over the past decades.

Thank you to all the generous hearted writers who have inspired me. To my University of Sydney Creative Writing teachers especially David Malouf, Kate Grenville and Sue Woolfe. Patti Miller for her inspirational work on memoir writing. All those wonderful and amazingly generous writers on the internet who share so much - a very special mention to Joanna Penn, Martha Alderson, Steven Pressfield, KM Weiland, Ellen Brooks and especially Liz Gilbert the most wonderful generous funny ambassador for embracing the creative life and 'just doing it'.

You will never know how much you have all helped me.
Thank you so much

Dear Readers and Writers,

I'm writing this to you in case you've ever wanted to write something yourself. If you've done it I absolutely applaud you because it's taken me decades to publish these stories!

I just wanted to share with you a bit of my experience in the hope that it might be helpful for those of you wondering whether to write or whether to publish. And that advice is:

Get Started Now

Don't wait!

If you stall, procrastinate, make excuses, put it off, wait till you 'have more' time, inspiration, money, training, confidence, experience, credibility, support, ideas then stop right now before you read this book, open your computer or pick up a pen and write one page about ABSOLUTELY ANYTHING and then read this book.

I ask you to do this because many many people who read (especially fiction) really want to write. I have read hundreds of novels in my life and never written one. I'm doing it now after decades of making the above excuses.

Remember you only have now. Now is the only time we all have. So now is the time to write. And when you start, your writing has a good chance of being clumsy and uninspiring. That's how the magic of creativity and learning works.

First you're clumsy, then you get better.

And better and better and it never stops.

But you have to do it.

Don't wait, Do it now.

Love and encouragement,

Linda

One Egg Or Two

I was the only patron in the *Ritz Café*. The lone waitress seemed impatient with me as if I was taking her away from more important tasks. She avoided eye contact, looking across the empty tables and chairs as if something of great fascination had captured her interest for the time it took me to read the menu and make a decision. When I indicated I'd made my selection she shifted her eyes, raised her pen and notepad to chest level and focused on the task of recording my choices. "Won't be long." With those words she was gone.

She probably thought I was lonely and would like to borrow her ear if she gave me half a chance. She seemed practiced at wordless signals of unavailability. At least she left me alone with my thoughts, which is a gift I'm sure she has no realization that she granted me.

Another traveller in need of sustenance entered my private world of thought. A woman in her fifties I would guess. Plump, using a walking stick painted, what can only be described as, 'hot pink.' I say fifties but her laboured walking aged her, perhaps she was only in her forties. Obviously dressed for comfort over style, her ample body was unrestrained in a loose top and a long skirt and her swollen cracked feet free to roam in a pair of misshapen sandals. Her hair outshone even her hot pink walking stick.

Wild and thick, seeming to defy gravity, shooting out from her scalp in all directions, multicolored, not in the usual sense that women thread color through their hair, but rather the first few inches from the roots were black then a few inches from the scalp it was orange. The ends, dark brown.

She had spent some minutes dragging the thick sandals along the ground until she reached the table next to mine. She pulled two chairs next to one another, hung her lurid stick over the back of one and lowered herself onto the two seats wriggling and wobbling, presumably to find a position in which the line where the two chairs met was in such a position that it caused her minimal discomfort.

I decided I would follow the example of the well practiced waitress and create around me an impenetrable barrier. I took a book from my briefcase and skewed my body away from the woman as subtly as I could. I opened the book in the middle, though I hadn't actually started reading it yet. I looked as if I was immersed in a gripping tale.

"'Scuze us." Her voice was as large as her body. It boomed across the small space separating our worlds. Every fibre of my body and mind wanted to continue reading. It was only some sense of propriety that said I could not so blatantly ignore another human being who had, as yet, caused me no harm. I raised my eyes from the lover's picnic and was jolted by the intensity of the dark eyes glowing in that overblown face which had lost all indication of structure and more resembled a bread bun than a human face. She was sweating profusely from her upper lip and forehead. Before I could answer she boomed a follow up. "What did you order? I can't decide."

"Just a pot of tea and a cheese sandwich."

"Sounds good to me." She turned her face towards the counter where the waitress had her back turned, keeping herself mysteriously occupied. "Love, love, I wanna order." The waitress turned, and sighing, walked towards her second customer of the day. "Cheese sandwiches and a pot of strong leaf tea, no bags." The waitress scribbled and left.

My eating companion patted the vacant chair at her table "Come and sit here, no sense in me leaning across, and I can see you're the type who's interesting."

I moved chairs, sensing that this was going to be one difficult situation to get out of. "Gwen, what's your name and what do you do?"

"I'm Peter and I..." She threw up her arms as if genuinely delighted by the sound of my name. "No, no, let me guess." She closed her eyes tightly, her face contorted with the effort. "Give me your hands, don't worry, give me your hands." She held hers out waiting to take mine. I placed mine into hers. She grasped them and squeezed her eyes tighter. I hoped she'd washed her hands some time that morning.

"Doctor. I can always tell - doctor's hands."

"Close." I should have said yes to have freed my hands from her clammy grip but I knew it wouldn't work. The waitress arrived and left our food with a look of poorly veiled contempt. Gwen let me go, leaned forward and whispered. "A doctor of animals. That's what you are."

"Is it that obvious?"

"To me it is. I can feel it."

3

"Really, that's astonishing."

"Don't make me blush. So you are an animal doctor aren't you?"

"Yes, yes actually I am." She smiled. Then she placed her palm across her sandwich and pressed hard. The bread sank to a thin trace of its former self. "This way the cheese blends into the bread, mmm." She picked up the flattened sandwich and took a large bite. I bit into mine with somewhat less enthusiasm. To my surprise it was very tasty. For a few moments we ate in silence. Gwen finished while I still had several mouthfuls to go. She rubbed her greasy hands together. "Get the left over fat into my skin. Cheaper than hand cream." She paused. "I want to ask you something."

"Go ahead."

"Do you know much about griffins?"

"Griffins?"

"I know, I know, well do you?"

"Not really except they seem to be on coats of arms." Gwen checked over her shoulder then leaned in and lowered her voice. Around her mouth was a shining ring of oil. "Ok, they have a lion's body and an eagle's head. The females have wings and the males have spikes growing from their shoulders."

"Curious, and so what's your interest in them?"

"No hang on, let me finish. They represent the two sides of our nature - good and evil, earth and heaven, that sort of stuff."

"But they're mythical, fantasy."

"Well, beasts from another realm."

"So what's your interest in them?"

4

"I've got one." She's mad, I thought. I knew it. "Have you now?" I knew I was sounding patronizing. "You think I'm mad don't you?" She stared straight into my eyes and she wasn't smiling.

"Possibly."

"Come to my place. Come on, eat up and come to my place."

"No, really, I have to go."

"It'll only take half an hour. I guarantee you won't regret it. I want you to look at her, you're a vet. I think she's sick."

"Gwen, this is outrageous. I'm sorry. I must get going. It's been really nice talking to you." I started to get up.

"Hey." Was all she said but the way she said it and the way she bored her gaze into my eyes I didn't move. "Come with me." There was something about her tone that made me doubt she was crazy after all.

"I dare you. Half an hour. You won't be disappointed." She was persistent. "So, are you game?" She was challenging me.

"OK, you show me your griffin then I can get back to work." I said trying to sound as unsurprised as I could. She heaved herself to her feet and called the waitress over. "Here take this for both us. Keep the change." The waitress smiled slightly and took the money over to the counter. Gwen and I were making for the door. "I'll need a lift." She said.

*****

I parked next to her house. Gwen struggled to get out of the car seat but by the time I'd reached the passenger side

5

she was standing. She reached the door of the house and showed me in. The air smelt strange. A tinge of a sort of musk. "In here." She pointed. I followed her into what was obviously a spare bedroom. The smell was so strong it caught in my throat. There was a single bed against one wall and that was it, nothing else.

On top of the bed was a creature asleep. It was about a metre long and curled up, as animals often do in sleep. I followed Gwen over and leaned across to get a good look. The room was full of sunlight so it was easy to see the creature. I don't know how to describe how I felt. I think my heart was racing, in fact I'm sure it was. I stared at the huge talons on the front feet, the back paws, the eagle's head, the feathered wings and furred rump ending in a long tail.

"Did you put something in my tea back there?"

"I told you."

"Gwen you're not serious. This thing's not real is it?" She didn't answer, she simply tapped the creature's head. The eye facing us opened. "No." Was all I could say.

"Oh yes, oh yes."

"Where did you get this?"

"Found it. Unusual things are attracted to me. Found it in a drain after a rainstorm."

"Where?"

"Can't remember now."

"Have you told anyone?"

"Course not, do you think I'm mad or something?" She chuckled. "Yes you do, of course."

"I don't know, I think maybe I'm mad, I'm having delusions right now."

"You know you're not."

"What are you going to do with it?"

"Her, Mimi's her name. Keep her of course. She's happy here. But I think she's a touch unwell."

"How would you know if a griffin's unwell?"

"I know her, I've had her since she was a baby. I know."

"And what am I supposed to treat a griffin with? Presuming that's why I'm here."

"Dunno, she's part eagle, part lion you choose."

"I'm not doing anything."

"Refusing to treat a sick animal?" She had me and she knew it. "Ok what's the problem?"

"She's lost her energy. She used to be jumpy and excitable and now this is all she does all day."

"How long?"

"The last week."

"Look, I have to go now but I'll come back tomorrow with a few things and have a good look at her."

"Ok, you'd better. I'm worried I'll never see you again, or you'll tell someone."

"You have my word." I looked into her eyes and we both knew I'd be back. I left the house and drove home. Bewildered is the only word I can think of to describe how I felt. All evening I spent researching griffins on the net. I really thought I was going out of my mind.

*****

I rang Gwen's doorbell three times before she answered. "Impatient? Don't you realize it takes me a while to get here." She waved her stick in explanation.

"How's the patient?" I enquired.

"You're not gonna believe it."

"No I probably won't, what?" She was opening the door to the griffin's room. It was still on the bed, still looking lethargic but with two shining green eggs, the color of agate, next to it on the bedcover. "Gwen don't joke with me."

"I'm not." She was pointing at the creature. "That's why she wasn't well. What do I do now? I'll have three bloody griffins. I can't manage that. You'll have to take them."

"Me? You are crazy."

"Well I'll have to smash the eggs then. No choice. I can't look after more than one." As she started towards the bed I had to stop her. "No, no I'll take them. I don't know what I'll do with them. Yes I do. I'll take them to the University."

"Don't you tell them you got them from me."

"Ok, Ok I'll tell them I found them in a drain near the railway station." As I approached the bed the griffin lifted its eagle head and moved its whole body. I spoke to the creature in a soft voice. "That's it, nice and calm, nice and calm." I turned to Gwen who was leaning over the mother and her eggs. "I really must go."

Gwen put the two eggs into a small box lined with rumpled paper and handed them to me. I took them and started to walk from the room. The griffin made a strange noise and stretched its body. It didn't seem to notice that the eggs had gone. I headed for the front door.

"I really appreciate you taking those for me. I didn't know what to do with them. I've got enough on my hands looking after her I couldn't look after griffin chicks as well."

"Look, I'll call in every so often and see how you're going with her OK."

"Oh you're such a lovely man. I could tell that from your hands."

"Yes, yes, good, now just be careful what you do with her. We don't know anything about these creatures or how to handle them."

"But I do, I've had her since she was a baby. I know her. Now get going but you must come back and see me and tell me what they say about the eggs."

"Yes I will. Don't see me out. I'm fine. Stay with Mimi." I rushed out, being really careful with the box. I put it on the floor of the car in front of the passenger seat so that it wouldn't fall if the car jolted. I started the engine and reversed slowly, anxious about the eggs. I packed a jacket I had on the back seat around the box to stop it moving. As I joined the traffic flow I drove slowly and was tailgated all the way home.

I turned carefully into my driveway and pulled up under the carport. I turned off the engine and leaned down to lift the box lid and check the eggs. As I stared down at the two green spheres I felt a wave of nausea hit my abdomen. There was an unmistakable crack across one shell and a pool of yellowish brown slime covering the bottom of the box.

"Jesus Christ." I couldn't believe what I was seeing. "What am I going to tell her?" I picked up the box, put the lid back on and carried it inside my house and into the kitchen where the light was brighter. I could see now that it

9

was more light brown than yellow, as slimy as any ordinary egg's contents with greenish streaks in the slime. I put the lid back on so that I couldn't see the sight any more.

*****

The following day I pulled into Gwen's street feeling the same nausea that I had felt the evening before when I looked at the mess inside the box. I pulled up at no. 15 and sat next to the kerb staring at the vacant piece of land in front of me. I realized I must have forgotten the number. I never do that. What was happening to me? I rechecked the map and noticed the house next door that I'd noticed yesterday because it had a bright orange front door.

I got out and walked onto the empty land. The grass was tall and coarse and there were no trees, nothing, just a 'For Sale' sign nailed onto a stake near the corner of the block. "You OK mate?" A middle aged man from the orange-doored house was leaning on the dividing fence. "Not a bad buy. Prices going up round here."

"Yes, not bad at all. Never had anything on it?"

"Not in the fifty one years I been here. Dunno about before that though. Interested?"

"I was looking for number 15 actually." I started striding towards the car. I needed to leave.

"That's 15 you're looking at. Could build a couple of townhouses on it."

"Are you absolutely sure that's 15?"

"Mate, I live in 13, have done for fifty one years, come on, I'm not losing my marbles yet." His tone was increasingly defensive. I needed to leave. "Yes, yes, thanks. Have a good afternoon."

"Yeh, mate and you." He walked back inside and closed the front door. I got in my car. My hand was trembling as I turned the key.

*****

I knew that when I got home there would be no box in the kitchen. What was going on? I decided I'd better take some time out, have a holiday, some time away. Something was seriously wrong with my mental state. It's a frightening feeling realizing that your mind has slipped from your control. That you've imagined a whole episode in your life and thought it was real. Driven to a place you thought existed. I tried to take slow deep breaths and focus on the here and now.

I turned on the kitchen light and looked around. The box was still there. I blinked hard and rubbed my eyes. I sensed that when I reached for it, it wouldn't be there. God, this is madness. This is what it actually feels like to start to lose touch with reality. I rubbed my hands against my shirt to get rid of the sweat. I reached for the box and felt the ridged cardboard against my fingertips. Then I lifted the lid. There, curled up the corner, was a tiny little creature with a beak, minute wings and a thread-like tail surrounded by broken egg shell.

First published in *Island* magazine.

The Upper Nepean

'*The Upper Nepean*' by Tasmanian artist, W C Pigeunit, painted in 1888, hangs in the Art Gallery of NSW, Sydney.

No one spoke to me on the bus coming in today. I think they all had the Monday blues. Must be the rain. Funny isn't it how all those people can be squashed together in a moving metal cage and not speak unless they know someone. In fact they try to avoid speaking. I've noticed. They read very intently or listen to music in those little headphones so that you'd feel rude speaking to them. Or they stare out the window with a vacant expression. Sometimes you meet their eyes in the reflection in the glass and they look away. Strange, looking into reflected eyes. Some pretend they're having a quick snooze. I say pretend because you can tell they're not asleep. They open their eyes every so often to check they're not near their stop.

Concentrate, focus on the painting and just let the pen flow across the page. Even in this tender light I feel jittery looking at that dark, brooding river with light cracking the clouds, struggling and just making it through. A shawl of mist hangs over the rock face, hiding its form, menacing, like it might ooze across the whole painting. The river's trapped between the cliffs. Will light break through the clouds and bounce and glitter on the surface and light up the cliffs or will the mist seep further into the gorge?

Yes, the sun will break through. The mist will retreat. The water will twinkle and the cliffs will warm. The strangling, seeping mist will be melted by the warmth - overpowered by the sunlight. No wonder the picture scares me. Evil lurks so powerfully there and it's only my belief that the light will triumph that settles my nerves. What was Piguenit's mood when he painted it? Did he feel the struggle I feel? Maybe not. On the surface it's a very calm scene.

When I'm home I'll add these notes to my folder. I've got one of those school folders with the rings and I put all my notes in it. I don't have a computer. I don't really want one either because I like writing by hand. Those screens and keyboards make everybody write the same. I don't like that. I like looking back at my notes and guessing what mood I was in just by looking at the writing.

I file my gallery notes every Monday evening and every so often I get the folder out and read them and try to arrange them into some sort of order. Hasn't worked yet but it will. I'm writing a book based on my ideas from the paintings. I've seen lots of books on what paintings are supposed to mean but these are my personal reactions. I choose one painting each visit to focus on. I try very hard not to look at the other paintings round about. I just stare at one painting. I don't time myself but now I find I've got a pretty good idea of about half an hour. Then I write whatever comes from the painting.

People in here sometimes look at me in a funny way. See I like beachcombing the charity shops and putting things together for effect. Today I'm wearing a purple velvet hat to which I've pinned a large yellow fabric flower I found last week. The hat had a bow on but I prefer the flower. My coat is one that someone else has worn for evenings out. At least that's what I think. It's been to many more exciting places than I ever have, I'm sure. It's black with a furry collar and a silver thread running through the fabric. Quite glam actually. But the shoes let me down. It's hard to find good shoes in charity shops so these black ones are heavy and flat and don't go with the coat. Can't wear heels because of my back.

"You alright there madam?"

"Yes I'm fine thanks, just fine." He's gone now. Probably thinks I'm a total nutter sitting here in my velvet hat with a notepad staring at a painting for half an hour. Boss probably told him to check out the old girl in the hat.

She likes it too. She's looking really carefully at it. Never seen her here before. Lovely hair. Expensive jacket. Probably thinks I'm a bag lady. "Excuse me, do you know anything about this painting?" Oh, didn't expect that. That type usually gives me a wide berth. "No sorry, 'fraid not. It just intrigues me."

"Yes, yes, it is, as you say, intriguing. That's a good word for it isn't it. Mysterious. Forbidding. Something rather dark about it isn't there?"

"Yeh, but look at that light eh. Just look at it behind those clouds. That's where the mystery is. Magical I reckon." She's smiling at my comment and she's gonna walk on nodding slightly. She doesn't want to hang around in case I start talking to her. So why did she speak to me to start with? Another mystery.

Here's a young'un. "Do you like it?" He's pretending he can't hear me. Too embarrassed to talk to an old dear in weird clothes. If I was forty years younger, then he would've answered. "Sort of mysterious isn't it?"

"Yes I guess you could say."

"Do you like it?" All I want to know is if he likes it or not. "Well, that's not really a question I ask of paintings myself. Do you *like* it?" Thinks he's pretty smart I'd say. Hasn't learned the simplicity of age. "Well, come on, what do you think of it then?" I still haven't got an answer. "Well Piguenit was a man of his time…"

"You know a lot about paintings then?"

"Oh I suppose you could say that. I read a lot. Self taught. Well, enjoy your day." Didn't answer my question. Didn't ask me my opinion. I notice these things. I bet he thinks I'm a stupid old woman with nothing better to do than sit alone in the art gallery and make a nuisance of myself.

Here comes another one. Goodness she looks upset. What should I say? I'm not very good at these things but she looks so upset poor dear, I should say something. "You OK love?" Oh no she's started crying. I've upset her. "Oh love, come on I'm sorry, I didn't mean to upset you."

"Look it's fine, it's not you. It's nothing to do with you, I don't even know you. It's me. I came here to get some peace but it doesn't work. Nothing works. There is no peace."

"Peace from what love?"

"From everything from all of them, from everyone."

"Everyone?"

"Yeh, you know the family, the kids. Everyone." Should I ask her something about her family or is that prying? But if I don't I look mean, like I don't care. But I don't even

16

know her. I'll have to say something. "Do you often come here?" That was really stupid, as if that's the thing to say to someone who's upset. "I mean where do you usually go when everyone's upset you?"

"Anywhere, anywhere where it's quiet and they won't follow me."

"So you like quiet?"

"I live for quiet. I live for escape from noise. Noise, day and night. I can't sleep for the noise in my head."

"In your head?"

"Yep my head rings at night with all the thoughts they're like dreams only I'm awake."

"You don't get much sleep?"

"Not with the kids waking up, him snoring and my head spinning."

"No I'm not surprised. So do you ever feel alright?"

"Only when I'm alone."

"You like that?"

"It keeps me alive."

"Really?"

"Yeh, sometimes I think I'll die if I don't get away. In fact I've thought that it might be nice, it'd be the quietest, calmest place. Have you ever thought about it?"

"What?"

"Death." God I'm silly of course she meant death. She wants to die. I know how she feels. No I don't. I'm eighty she's about thirty. I don't know how she feels. "Yes, yes of course I've thought about it. I'm getting on, as you can see, so I get to thinking about it often these days."

"And?"

"I wonder where and when I'll go."

"Do you really?"

"Yes I mean I come here a lot and I sometimes wonder what'd happen if I just keeled over on one of these seats and that was it. Look I've gotta get going love. You feeling a bit better now?"

"I guess. Are you lonely?"

"Look, yes, I get lonely. Who wouldn't? I live alone. I have no children or grandchildren."

"What does it feel like?"

"What does what feel like? Living alone?"

"No being lonely?" This is too much. She's getting annoying now.

"I really must go."

"No please, just a few minutes. That's all."

"Well not long."

"No just tell me what it's like to feel lonely."

"Right. Well, it's hard to describe. It's sort of empty."

"Where?"

"What do you mean where?" I'm sounding annoyed now. "Where, in your head, in your stomach?"

"Where? Well in here somewhere I suppose, please…"

"Does it hurt?"

"No"

"It doesn't ache?"

"No, I really must go now." She's one of those persistent ones.

"Well what does it feel like?"

"I said it feels empty."

"What does empty feel like."

"It feels like, it feels like a little kid."

"Yeh?"

"I suppose. I don't know. But you know when you see pictures of sad little kids sucking their thumbs on those charity ads. It feels like that." My throat's getting tight, and achey. I'm going. "I must go."

"Oh must you?"

"I'm sorry. Please, look, I must go."

"Let me come with you. I've upset you. Sorry, it's my fault. I'm sorry honestly." She's putting her arm round my shoulder. I'm going outside I'll feel stronger in the fresh air and the light. She's standing looking at me. Why can't she just go away?

"Let me get you a cup of tea. I insist. Do you take milk?"

"Yes, yes, milk please."

"Won't be long. You just stay there and don't move. Just relax. I'll be back." I'm going. Good, she's gone. A walk across the park, that's what I need. Please don't follow me. Just leave me. Just don't follow me. I'm an old woman I want to be alone. Loneliness doesn't hurt me now. I like being alone. What's she shouting?

She's standing there with two cups of tea. She looks a bit silly. I don't care. I'll just keep walking. I won't turn and look at her. If I walk as quickly as I can I'll be at the bus stop soon. The sun's breaking through the clouds. It's warm on my back. I was right about the painting, that the light would win out.

First Published in *Linq* Magazine.

The Sewing Class

Would she ever get used to waking alone in bed after all those years of being used to having another body close by? She had come to feel that one of the best reasons for being partnered was to have someone to sleep with. Literally. Not the sex 'sleep with,' but literally to sleep with. To leave each day holding someone in the dark silence and to wake each morning and find them still there.

She snuggled under her doona, fending off the approaching day. At eight she gave in, got up and turned on the radio to fill the ringing silence with a familiar impersonal voice. Someone telling her about traffic snarls and overnight family dramas made her feel part of other people's lives again. After toast and coffee she surveyed her diary, bought after deciding she must put some structure back in her life, some limits on her endless time. She'd set a self-imposed timetable. Thursday morning was her beach walk.

Ben used to get her to go walking with him which she always resisted until his enthusiasm broke through and they'd head out for two hours even in the winter cold and rain. He'd tell her to leave the umbrella in the car and run to get warm, while feeling the cold rain on her hair and face. They would run the whole length of the beach in the pouring rain and he was right, it wasn't cold at all. It was glorious! When they arrived at Bradley's Point he would jump around dripping wet as she laughed at him from under the overhanging rocks. Back home they'd towel each other's hair, wrap themselves in old dressing gowns and drink hot tea.

*****

This morning the ocean was pulsing. Leaving her running shoes well up the beach she raced to the edge and let the freezing water tickle her calves. Her body tightened with the shock and she jumped up and down on the spot trying to move her blood through her veins. Alone on the beach, she stared out at the horizon. If I swam as far as I can see I wonder if I'd just see the same vast empty expanse again and another distant meeting point with the sky?

So much space.

So much emptiness.

To try and stop shivering she started jogging along the damp sand. The movement warmed her, the pounding of her feet and the rhythmic sound of the waves lulled her until she was anywhere, everywhere, everything - sand, water, wind. All of it. She jogged the length of the beach to Bradley's Point but didn't linger there.

*****

"You need to meet people, it'll help, I know, I've been through it. You can't brood, Worst thing you can do. You've got to get out of yourself. Look love I know how hard it is. When Mark left I thought I'd never manage.

But you do. You do." An impatient child's voice demanded Rosie's attention. "Gotta go, that'll be Nathan. Do as I say love, get out alright?" Charlotte smiled and nodded. She never argued with Rosie. It would take more energy than she had at the moment. Raising five children on her own meant Rosie had seemingly unlimited knowledge about life. There was nothing Rosie Cartwright didn't know something about.

The two women spent more time together than Charlotte thought advisable but Rosie was hard to contain. When Rosie was in Charlotte's house she seemed to expand into every corner, every private space and even then when Rosie had gone it felt as if some part of her stayed there. *Bold and Daring* fragrance filled the rooms and Charlotte had to open windows, even in winter, to let Rosie out.

"Just the thing, thought of you straight away. You said you used to sew. Look, '*Sewing classes for beginners or experienced*' and it's only fifty dollars. You'll enjoy it, honestly. If I had a machine I'd come with you. Ring them today because some of their courses get full up pretty quick." Rosie's long index finger was jabbing at the page.

"Thanks Rosie, I don't know what I'd do without you to organize me."

"Love, I don't know either, organising's my talent, I don't have other talents, like artistic or brain wise but I can organise. I'll call in tomorrow and you can tell me what they said."

****

23

The following Thursday, Charlotte was introducing herself to eight local women sitting behind sewing machines in a primary school classroom. The teacher, Raylene was obviously practiced at making leisure classes fun and Charlotte felt herself relaxing as she re-learned the basics of cutting and sewing. At the end of class Charlotte lingered, pretending to sort out her bag as the other students filed out. Raylene was packing up her gear and cleaning the whiteboard.

"Charlotte, what do you think you'll tackle? You said you'd done quite a bit of sewing."

"Yes, I used to do a lot actually. I started out making clothes for the kids but when they left and I had more time I started doing other things. I haven't done any lately."

"Why did you stop?"

"I moved, away from the city, I needed to leave, my husband left...suddenly."

"Oh, I'm so sorry, I had no idea."

"No, of course, it's fine. So I sort of haven't got back into it, but a neighbour thought I might enjoy this."

"And did you?"

"It was wonderful actually. After I relaxed I started to feel like I'd never stop. I wish it wasn't a week before I come again."

"Look Charlotte do some at home. Anything, just buy some fabric and let yourself go. Bring in what you start and you can carry on working on it next week."

"I will, yes, I definitely will - get me out of myself."

"It might help, I don't know, look can I just say that I know it must be really hard for you."

"It'll get better, especially if I find something to get my teeth into, I'll do what you said, and thanks for the class."

By the time she was back in her car Charlotte felt lighter and more energetic than she had in months. She wanted the week to pass in an instant so that she would be back in class again.

She awoke damp with sweat the next morning so reached to turn the electric blanket off and go back to sleep. She had dreamt about Ben. She couldn't remember the dream but it had left her feeling alone and exhausted. The joy of the night before had vanished. Her head was aching and the memory of the class now made her feel nervous. Bloody Rosie and her stupid idiot idea. I don't want to 'get out and meet people' I want to be left alone. I'm not getting up today and I'm not going back to that class.

By ten a.m. she was desperately thirsty so forced herself up to make a pot of tea. Crisp winter sun was lighting up the dusty surfaces but also suffusing the place with a 'you-can't-stay-in-bed' energy. After a long shower she felt better. She felt stronger and the memory of the class was more balanced. 'I did well actually, I got myself there and I spoke to the other women and Raylene. Yes I did well.' She said to herself.

While drying her hair she noticed the boxes on top of the wardrobe. Ten boxes containing her life, high up, out of reach, unless she made an effort to get them down. Books, letters, photos, souveniers of holidays with Ben. And, the last garment she'd made for herself - the evening jacket for the Opera Gala - was packed away in one of those boxes. It was a struggle but she reached the one marked 'Evening clothes.' She remembered packing away her best clothes,

25

knowing that at Seacliff she wouldn't need them. Anyway they would remind her too much of special times.

She opened one of the top flaps of the box. Her black cocktail dress. Doubt if I'll fit into that now. Next was the Opera Gala jacket. She lifted it out carefully and laid it on the bed. Had she really made that? She gazed at the gold beaded, Italian silk. The exquisite cut, the perfect finish. The plain, black silk cuffs.

She remembered the wonderful little fabric shop that sold the European silk off-cuts. The owner, always in black, always eager to show her another bolt that had come in. Their shared passion. The smell of new fabric. The untidy shelves, the chinking of the scissors on the counter, the rushed drive home. The staying up till two or three in the morning till her neck ached so much she was forced to crawl as quietly as possible into bed next to Ben.

She'd caught up on sleep while he was at work. She worked better alone at night. Darkness and silence focused her. That delicious passion, that intoxicating feeling, knowing that it was going to be beautiful and admired and people would ask her where she bought it and she would say 'I made it myself' and they would gasp in disbelief.

"Will you stop your fighting." A car door slammed. Rosie and the kids were home next door. Distracted, she put down the jacket, refolded it, repacked the box and returned it to the top of the wardrobe.

Charlotte felt a little reticent about bringing out the fabric at the next class. She feared some of the women in the class who were making sensible blouses and tops for their children might not understand.

"Ok, out with your work, let's get going." Raylene clapped her hands. As bags rustled and machines were threaded, Charlotte unwrapped her cut pieces. The red damask looked an even richer ruby color than in the shop and the gold thread flickered in the overhead lights. Raylene gasped.

"Charlotte, where did you get that divine fabric?"

"I made a little trip into the city this week and saw a friend of mine. I used to buy fabric from her. Italian." Raylene made her way to Charlotte's table and other women were craning to have a look and making comments.

"Must've cost a fortune."

"What are you making with that?"

"Who's it for?" Feeling a little flustered, Charlotte attempted to answer their questions. Raylene picked up a cut-out sleeve.

"This is the most beautiful fabric imaginable Charlotte. Show me what you're making please." Hesitantly Charlotte handed Raylene the pattern.

"Is it for a special occasion?"

"Yes, it is, a very special occasion." Charlotte didn't elaborate and Raylene didn't ask any more. "You will look absolutely gorgeous, believe me." Empathy flashed between the two women.

When the course of classes finished Charlotte was about half way through the dress. She had been taking it slowly and not working on it much between classes. She preferred to sew in company, listening to the women as they worked, talking and moaning about their husbands and children, making jokes and telling funny stories. She said very little and suspected that she was seen as a bit aloof but the women seemed to accept her and were friendly and pleasant. Each week they gathered around her to check the progress of the beautiful garment and try to find out, without success, where it would be worn.

She had exactly a week to finish the dress at home. She woke earlier than usual and skipped lunch to finish the beading around the yoke, which took hours and left her with sore and sometimes bleeding fingers. When completed, the dress was hung on a satin padded hanger in the bedroom waiting for the following Sunday. Charlotte would stand and gaze at the rich red fabric and the exquisite beading, a sweeping neckline and pin tucks down the bodice. Charlotte had to admit she was surprised. She found herself smiling at this glorious creation of hers. She felt almost happy.

The project had focused her so intensely that she had even found the strength to control Rosie's intrusions. Rosie had found numerous excuses to call - to borrow milk, to bring her the mail or her empty garbage bin - and to ask if she was OK.

"Charlotte, are you sure you're alright? It's not like you, you're usually so friendly. I'm a bit worried, I've read about people who start not going out, it can get worse you know. How about just a quick coffee?"

"Look Rosie, I'm fine, I really am, I'm just busy."

"How can you be busy when you weren't busy before?"

"I can't explain. I'll have a bit more time soon, but not as much as I used to have. I promise, I'll have a cup of coffee with you next week."

"OK love, if you insist you're alright. But if you feel like you need a bit of company just call won't you? Don't forget now."

"No I won't. Thanks Rosie."

She took the whole of Sunday afternoon to get ready. She bathed in scented oil and slowly creamed her body. She washed her hair, then scooped it up loosely, not in the usual neat twist. She applied full make up and sprayed herself with Chanel No. 5, purchased especially for the occasion. While preparing herself she had been checking on an exquisite chicken in wine cooking slowly and becoming increasingly fragrant.

Before dressing, she wrapped herself in her dressing gown and set the table for one, adding a lilac scented candle and a small bunch of pale pink rose rosebuds in the crystal vase they had bought in Prague on their honeymoon. She checked the meal. It was ready and she served herself on a china plate from the best dinner service they'd always reserved for special guests. Placing the meal in the oven to keep warm, she returned to the bedroom to dress.

Black patent strap sandals and sheer stockings. Her treasured French silk underwear and the dress. Taking it from the hanger, she unzipped it slowly and placed it carefully over her head so as not to disturb her hair. She eased it over her now-generous hips and zipped it up. The fit was perfect. The low bodice showed her smooth neck and the crystal beads shimmered in the dim light of the bedroom. The luscious damask sheathed her body and showed off her now curvaceous figure. She looked in the full-length mirror and smiled. Billy Holiday's voice sang of love and heartache. She unhooked the phone and dimmed the lights. Placing her plate of fragrant food before her she unfolded her napkin and placed it on her lap. The voice recorder was next to her plate. She switched the record button on.

"Ben, darling. Today is our 22nd wedding anniversary and I'm celebrating our life together in style. I'm not going to speak for long and when I stop I'll savor my meal, have a liqueur and retire. Ben, my life with you did not end two years ago, I have lived with you ever since, every minute of every single day. After tonight I will be officially free to start again. I don't know what my new life will bring. I will always love you, I'll never know why you left but I must let you go now, forgive you and start again. Good bye Ben and thank you for the good times."

Charlotte touched the 'Stop' button. She removed the micro-tape and placed it in the silver gift box she'd bought especially for the occasion and tied it with a silver ribbon. It would fit nicely into the corner of the box containing the Opera Gala jacket. When the evening was over she would pack the dress in with it and return the box to the high shelf.

She picked up her fork and began to eat.

A Companion To Owls

I am a brother to dragons, and a companion to owls. Job 30: 29

Joseph Dwight Robbins was jobless and spent a lot of time in bed. He had a cash flow problem. He didn't have any. After rent there was only enough to buy a few tins of generic brand food. Joseph's 'home' was *Windsor Apartments*, a boarding house of sorts ruled over by a Mrs. Joan Jeffries - one of those late middle-aged women who straddle the boundary between the sexes and it remained a mystery to Joseph as to which category she best fitted. Joan Jeffries had a deep, raspy voice, chin hair and broad shoulders. What Joseph found most disturbing however was her enormous breasts almost bursting out of her faded cotton blouse which she would wear for an entire week, even in the sultriest of summers.

Three days ago Mrs. J. as she referred to herself, had knocked on Joseph's door, startling him as he never had visitors. He always handed Mrs. J. his rent to prevent her calling to collect it. He heaved his body out of bed and shuffled across his room. Hurrying didn't suit Joseph these days.

"Who is it?" he called. He wasn't opening the door to anyone he didn't know.

"You know who it is Jo. I need to talk."

"I've paid." Joseph called out, hoping this would send her away.

"It's not that, let me in." Joseph fiddled with the rusted security chain until the door opened. The breeze from the open window in his room sucked the smoke from Mrs. J's cigarette into his face. He waved it away. She didn't apologise.

"I need help." This statement launched Mrs J. into a mucous-filled coughing fit. Joseph stared at the floor in an effort to avoid the onslaught. Thumping her chest as she recovered she blurted, "There's an owl in my kitchen. I don't know what to do."

"Right," was all Joseph could think of saying.

"I know what you're thinking, all that grog's done her brain in at last. Well it hasn't – there's an owl in my kitchen, sure as I'm standing here." Joseph wasn't sure about her brain or the grog or the owl but he knew the quickest way to get her to leave was to sort it out.

He stepped into the hall next to Mrs. J. and pulled the door closed behind him. The narrow, greasy space didn't offer much in the way of standing room for two. No matter how much Joseph squirmed and shuffled he couldn't avoid being in contact with Mrs. J's fleshly bosom. 'Bosom' rather than 'breasts' seemed appropriate to describe the shelf of flesh between Mrs. J's armpits and waist.

Extracting herself from this excruciating situation, Mrs J. wheezed her way downstairs to her private ground floor quarters, followed by a reluctant Joseph. She let him in first. "Have a look, see what you think." Her grubby hand felt inside the door and flicked on the light. There was so much furniture and clutter in her living area that Joseph wasn't

32

sure where to look. "There, see, look." She was jabbing a chubby finger in the direction of the window where a magnificent bird with huge dark eyes was perched on the back of a less than magnificent chair.

Joseph had seen few owls in his life - maybe two in fifty-five years, so the sheer weirdness of the situation was what struck him. Here in a grimy, sleazy, inner-city boarding house owner's living room was a creature of such immense majesty and mystery it made Joseph gasp. It didn't move. Joseph was sure it was startled. "What am I supposed to do with it?" He whispered.

"I don't know but it gives me the creeps. Look at it. It doesn't move. It's so big."

"I think it's scared."

"Are they dangerous? I mean, they kill things with those claws don't they?"

"Yes." Joseph replied "But it's not going to kill anything here." Mrs J. let out a sigh of relief leading to another coughing bout.

"What shall we do with it?" She asked when she'd recovered.

"Maybe just open the window and it'll go out."

"How'd it get in?" She asked Joseph as if assuming Joseph would know. "I don't know but I think two of us might scare it, how about I just see what I can do, eh?" Joseph said, hoping desperately she would leave him alone with the owl.

"Ok, I'll go in the bedroom and have a lie down and leave you to it." Mrs. J. shuffled off into the only other room and shut the door rather too loudly. The owl didn't respond. Its unblinking gaze was starting to unnerve Joseph.

He sat down on the misshapen sofa and tried to breathe slowly and calmly and be as still as the owl. He realised in that moment that he'd reached fifty-five and knew virtually nothing about owls. His ignorance had caught up with him and now, faced with this beautiful and unnerving wild creature, he was unable to do anything because he didn't know anything. He knew nothing about its behaviour, its habits or its responses. He could've lived his entire life and never have had a thought about these wondrous creatures. He was quite overcome by that prospect.

He sat as silent as the owl for a few more moments. All he could think of doing was ringing up a wildlife rescue group to come and take it away to some forest and let it go.

There was a grubby phone on Mrs. J's table near the owl. Joseph stood up as slowly and smoothly as he could so as not to startle the bird. He leaned over and picked up the smeared handset and dialled directories, holding the foetid mouthpiece as far away from his own mouth as possible. After being given a number he rang, *Rescue Them Now*. A brusque woman took the address and details, saying, "Someone'll be round soon so don't do anything to make it panic."

He replaced the handset and continued to sit still. He thought that opening a window close by would give the owl the freedom to fly away should it want to. He realised what an obvious solution this was and this gave him an excuse to berate himself for being so stupid in the face of the obvious.

Joseph got up as slowly as he could and crept towards the window above the kitchen sink. He was surprised that the owl didn't turn its head as he walked past. He fiddled with the rusty fastener and pushed the window open as far as it would go. Just as he was trying to push it even further he sensed movement behind him, then the owl's wings brushed his head as it flapped frantically in an attempt to fly through the opening. Joseph ducked instinctively and the creature struggled through the confined space and took flight. By the time Joseph leaned over the sink to look out and up, he could no longer see it. All that was left was a large splodge of sticky owl dropping on the window ledge and a feather in the sink.

Joseph stood for some moments, staring up at the sky almost willing himself to see the bird flying free, but he couldn't. It was gone. He felt moved, almost teary. For a few minutes he'd shared his life with a mysterious creature of the night. He didn't even know what type of owl it was. Suddenly, like a wave of nausea, the sheer vastness of his own ignorance struck him with full force. It was more of a shock to him than either the presence of the owl or its sudden departure. He felt in that single moment an unnerving sense of panic as it dawned on him. He knew so little. He had been given so much time. He had lived alone for the last ten years since Leila left him. He hadn't worked. He'd had hours, days, weeks, months, years to himself in which he could have found out anything he wanted to know and he hadn't. He had filled his mind with the trivial details of existence. He felt a deep sense of loss and rising panic.

Returning to the present moment he was aware that he was still standing in Mrs J's sordid living room and that she was still in her bedroom thinking there was an owl in her kitchen. He could not face her. Not now. She must have fallen asleep or she would be calling out wanting to know what was happening. Joseph found a used envelope and a pen and scrawled 'Flew out of window. Ring this number and tell them not to bother.'

He didn't close the window - fume-ridden city air smelt better than the stink of unwashed body, fried eggs and stale cigarette smoke. He closed Mrs J's front door as quietly as possible and returned to his now fresh-by-comparison little living space, closed his window and took to his bed.

It was 11am and he had just encountered and set free a wild and beautiful creature. He had done something! But there under his cheap and cheerful doona he pondered. What had he done yesterday morning? He'd woken early as usual with the light streaming through his unlined curtains at dawn. He'd stayed in bed with his mind blank except for the awareness in his body of wanting to go to the toilet. After attending to that he'd made a cup of tea. Then he'd returned to bed to lie and drift in and out of sleep for the next hour or so until he was again driven out of bed by physical need - this time the rumbling of his stomach. That was about ten o'clock. Then what had he done?

*****

"You there? Jo, where's the owl?" Mrs J. was banging with her pudgy fist and the door was rattling in its frame with the sheer power behind those knuckles. Joseph opened up and Mrs J. bulldozed her way in. "What did you do? Come on, you left without telling me."

"You were asleep."

"Yes well, tell me now."

"I opened the window."

"I saw that." She muttered sarcastically, "but what did you *do*? It's gone."

"I opened the window." He repeated, wanting her to go so that he could have a sleep.

"So, it's really gone?" She sounded disappointed. Joseph had a silly thought that maybe she'd stolen it from the zoo. The spectre of Mrs J. charging through the turnstile at the zoo with a zipped-up travel bag containing a stunned owl, made him smile. "How did you get it out?"

"It flew out."

"Don't be difficult, Jo." She seemed exasperated. "I want to know exactly what you did to get it to fly out." Her blotchy face was tilted back in all its puffed glory, pleading with him to tell her how he'd done what he'd done. "Mrs J. I'll tell you what I did. I walked across to the window right." He thought he'd act out the whole episode for her so he got up, walked over to his window and tugged at the fastener. The window flew open and a warm breeze blew in. "I leaned over your sink like this and I opened the window."

"Right, yes, I know, I hadn't got round to those dishes, I was tired this morning." She squirmed a little, remembering the food-caked plates in the sink. "I pushed open your window and I was just about to turn round and the owl started flapping its wings and next second it was gone. Just like that."

"Just like that."

"Nothing to it."

"Well thanks, really. I did get a shock, I mean it was just there. I don't know how it got in."

"Do you only have one window like me?' Joseph asked. She nodded. "And I opened it." He stated.

"That's what you just said."

"So it was closed before that."

"Always closed, can't stand the traffic."

"How did it get in then, if you never open your window?"

"Never." She blinked but stayed silent. They were oddly bound together by their confusion.

"I need to sit down." She set herself down heavily on Joseph's only armchair. He imagined the strain on the broken leg at the back. She leaned forward and Joseph tried not to look at her well-worn cleavage. "I had my breakfast as usual and I went into the bedroom for my cigs. Always have a smoke after breakfast to relax me for the day. You know, get's me ready to face things. I came out of the bedroom and it was there."

"Just there."

"Yep, perched there. Thought I was going gaga I did so I stopped and looked at it and saw it was real. I got scared then and I came up to you."

"And I came down and let it out of the window that was closed all morning."

"Because…"

"Of the traffic noise. Well I'm stumped. Must've been a ghost." Joseph laughed.

"Don't Jo, that's mean. I'll be scared now."

"There'll be some explanation."

"I need a smoke. I'll have to go. I'm really nervous now though, going to my place."

"It's OK, it's gone."

"Yeh, but if it got in with the window closed what if I go down and it's there again? Or what if something else has come in?" She was frowning now and looking more wizened than usual.

"OK, I'll come down with you, but I'm not staying. I'll just check the place."

"Oh thank you Jo, thank you, you're so kind." He followed her down the stairs. At her door she gave Joseph the key so that he could go in first. He pushed open the door, looked around, checked the bedroom, embarrassed by the stale female smell and tried not to notice the grubby underclothes strewn across the bed. "Looks fine, must fly." They laughed together at his unintended joke. He hadn't laughed with Mrs. J. before. A squeamish intimacy hung between them.

"Thank you so much Jo. I can't thank you enough." She was smiling as if she actually liked him. She waved and as she closed the door she winked at him. He didn't know how he felt about that.

Standing in the hallway, Joseph was about to climb the stairs back to his flat. He thought he might go back to bed to recover from the whole exercise. But he didn't. Instead he walked down the hallway, stepped out into the street and started walking. He didn't need to go out for food or anything. This was the first time he'd gone out for a walk for its own sake for longer than he could remember.

Out there in the light and air he noticed how busy the street was. How many people were out and about, living their lives, going about their daily business. He looked up at the blue expansive sky. For the first time in as long as he could remember he just wanted to be outside. He started to walk along the street. He didn't know where he was going and he was very surprised to notice that he didn't care.

First Published in the *London Journal of Fiction*

Meander

She likes curtains. She can choose which parts of her life she wants people to see. She can hide behind them if she needs to. On any given day she can decide whether or not to open them. If they stay closed people will wonder why she hasn't opened them. She doesn't care. She can't remember the last time she cared what anyone thought about her. It took her and Rudi the whole weekend to hang the new damask curtains in the two front rooms.

She'd only had five hours sleep and woke with a heavy headache. She stayed in bed in the darkened room for a while. Maybe later she'd sit on the sofa on the veranda in the fresh air. She'd gaze across the valley towards the outline of the coarse black mountain, its sheer drop silhouetted against the white autumn sky. *Starkey's Bluff*, marked on the map at 1576 metres.

'Bluff - a headland with perpendicular broad face.' The Concise Oxford Dictionary.

At any moment a shawl of mist could hover around the bluff then settle for a while, obscuring it completely and utterly. If you didn't know, you could arrive in the valley and leave again without knowing *Starkey's Bluff* even existed. She smiles. Somehow, she thought, the Bluff would probably like it that way - living up to its name. Dangerous and beautiful, tempting people to try and reach the top, many would fail, some tragically. But it reminds her that she has chosen life. The movement inside her bulging belly proving she had been right in her choice to live that night.

*****

That night she had stood with her toes just inches from the cliff edge staring out to the horizon, her hands firmly pushed down into the pockets of her sensible navy blue jacket. I should surrender and drop to the rocks below she thought. I will discover then how resistant my bones are to shattering and splintering when smashed against solid ancient objects. How easy it is to destroy oneself. One jump, one slip, murdered by gravity. Or maybe I would float and fly like a seagull or a hang glider. To try something, to take a risk, to be as free as a... and I will pay with my life to taste absolute freedom for a few seconds. It will be the last thing I do, suspended for a nano-moment before the plunge and the fresh air from the sea rushes past me - for how long? How long will it take? Five seconds? Six seconds?

His voice was calm. "Hey, careful, don't move." Rudi. What does he want? "You OK?" He approached, frowning. "Aren't you freezing?"

"No, just looking. Isn't it beautiful tonight?"

"And dangerous." He laughed. "Like some o' you women." He grasped her elbow. They turned and trudged through the thick coarse cliff grass. The wind reached into her bones like icy spears.

"Gotta be careful standing there you know, gets slippery this time o' year."

"I'm Ok Rudi, thanks." She patted his arm. He didn't speak again. The wind was stronger. It was dangerously dark. At the car park he spoke again. "See you round."

"I'll give you a lift. It's very cold." She said.

"Nup, like walkin,' always have." He left, long hair streaming out behind, hunched over in that old black coat. Dickensian. Would scare a lot of people. But in reality you can't tell who to be scared of, she knew that only too well.

*****

The first time she'd shared a sleeping bag with Rudi it had seemed odd to be in a zipped-up cocoon with a man she'd only met an hour before. Intimate, claustrophobic even. She'd tried to push down her side of the bag to feel less constricted. Rudi was asleep with the bag pulled up covering the bottom third of his face.

She'd thought he was asleep. "Having a bit of trouble there?" His voice was clear in the night air.

"No, no I can sleep anywhere believe me." She knew that he knew she was faking.

"I gave up pillows. Here try this." He handed her a small oblong cushion he'd been using. "For your neck. Sleep well." She held it to her face. The scent from the cushion was familiar, sandalwood with a hint of something fresh - lemon or lime maybe.

Rudi fell asleep. She was amused that he didn't seem to care that he had no idea who he was sleeping with. This stranger and sharer of his sleeping space who'd drifted into his life that evening and said she had nowhere to stay - said she'd been away from city life for a long time and had only just returned. He didn't ask questions, just said if she needed somewhere to stay that was fine but that she'd have to share his sleeping bag on the floor as he hadn't bought a bed yet. Hadn't got round to it. She'd told him everything in the next two hours - he was that sort of guy. He seemed nice enough. She had nothing to lose. As she lay there listening to his breathing, she knew that tomorrow she would ask him to help her find a place to live. Somewhere quiet. She didn't expect she would be sharing it with him but life is an unpredictable thing.

*****

The first thing she'd done after moving in together was to name the cottage. She had carved a crude sign on a piece of pine planking and nailed it next to the front door. "*Meander,* isn't it a great name? From now on I'm going to meander through life."

"No better place to do it." Rudi was attempting to put up a hammock between two veranda poles. "Hammock's a good name too don't you think? I'm gonna lie in this for the rest of my life." She punched him playfully.

"I think people name their houses because they want to claim them as their own. Don't you think so?" He winked and she smiled back at him and laughed at him fighting with the hammock as he tried to climb into it.

She now had a space on this earth where she could truly be herself. It would be like that now, here, in this modest timber cottage facing the Bluff. This house would be her place to share with someone she loved and a new someone

44

that her body was creating. She couldn't believe she'd come this far and been so blessed. This is my escape from all that I won't or can't face. A place I will only share with those of my choosing. Did that include Mother? She must take Rudi to visit Mother and tell her the news. She must. But not right now. She needed to settle in first.

She wondered if people in Rossvale would remember her face from the newspapers.

"What do you think Rudi? Do you think they'll recognise me, put two and two together?"

"They might think it's quite cool to have an ex-con living amongst them."

"Oh don't be ridiculous."

"No, seriously, marginalised people are considered cool these days."

"Stop it you're being patronising."

"No I'm not, it's like tatts and piercings, once marginal and unacceptable to most people, then cool, now commonplace, soon to be passé."

"Maybe in the inner city but not in Rossvale."

"I think you might be misjudging people here."

"I don't think so."

"Anywhere so far off the beaten track probably has people living in it with, let's say, interesting stories to tell."

"So I'll be among friends eh." He smiled at her comment, stubbed out his cigarette, walked to her, held her tightly and kissed her neck.

"Yeh, frontier country. That's what this is."

*****

Since moving to Rossvale she was much more aware of sound. Maybe that happened during pregnancy. Or maybe the soundscape of this place was so utterly different from the city and Milldale that her brain was adjusting and in the process had become much more sensitive to the noises around her. She noticed the individual calls of birds she didn't know the names of yet. She didn't know what they looked like either and didn't really care. There was plenty of time for that. All she knew was that she loved their sounds, clear in the morning air.

And it was absence she noticed too. Absence of the interminable noise of people shouting, doors clanging and slamming, keys rattling. The institutional noises she'd grown so used to. Here she heard a single vehicle as it crunched its way through the gravel of the unmade roads, quiet at first, then louder, then falling away again. She would try and identify the point at which she ceased to hear it altogether. She hadn't been able to yet.

Some days the Bluff scared her. Storm energy scared her. The thunder rolled, gentle at first, a heaving mass rumbling across the sky and as the pressure built and the storm gathered, changing from a roll to a roar and eventually a crack. The clouds would split open and discharge their energy in a white hot fork. When she was little someone told her that it was only the thunder she could hear and that lightening was silent. That made it more scary - that lightening could streak down to anywhere on the ground with no warning - you couldn't hear it coming, there was no escape, you didn't know where its next bone-melting flash might hit.

On days when the Bluff disappeared in grey swirls and the wind rattled the tin roof, it reminded her of the weekly ferry trip across the straits to the island where her Father lived. She and her Mother would make the trip no matter what. Her stubborn Mother would never give up trying to make things better. They would huddle together in the centre of the old boat as far as possible from the doors, which never seemed to fully close, letting in knife blades of sea air.

Even then her Mother would be cheerful. Sadness, her Mother said, was like a deadly disease that you had to fight and never let it get a hold because once it did there was no going back. Going back to what? She had wondered about that as a fifteen year old.

"You've got to be happy like me and how do I do it?" Her mother had held her close as the ferry ploughed through the waves, the hot oily smell of the engine making her feel nauseous. "Willpower. I will myself. Every morning when I wake up I thank God I'm alive and to show him just how grateful I am I pull back the curtains, open the window, no matter what the weather, and I breathe deeply of the fresh air of a new morning, a new start. Whatever happened yesterday is past. Today is new, a new start, a new life." Yes, her Mother's curtains were always open from morning to night. Nothing to hide in her house.

She'd tried to keep her Mother's hopeful words in her mind during her time in Milldale. It was hard. It was a long time. Mother was kidding herself, you can't just cut off from everything, go to sleep, wake up and it's all OK. How had her mother done it for all those terrible years before the separation and had she been able to stick to her philosophy after that night?

*****

The ferry would lurch and sway and the windows would be covered with frothy splashes. As the bow cut through the freezing waves it would seem as if the whole structure of the vessel was heaving and groaning and with the next crash would be dashed to pieces, seats and passengers sprayed across the ocean in slow motion before disappearing into the boiling surface.

Then they would arrive at the island. Its peace and beauty were deceiving. Who would have thought that in a place of patchwork fields and neat homesteads lived a being so volatile, so troubled, so ill at ease with the world that within his private universe there existed a space filled only with nameless fear? Nothing safe, warm and secure could enter his space of terror and unknowing. Sometimes when they arrived at the paint peeling door of her Father's grubby house she wished that just one wave had been too powerful, that her imagination could be transformed into reality and that they had never reached the island.

But it was never so, for years she endured the thundering voice echoing through the almost empty rooms, the threats, the fists, until that day when, at fifteen years old something in her reached its limit, smashed through her defences and a strength she had not known she possessed was set free.

The headlines condensed the horror of that night into four simple words: '*Teenager Attacks Monster Dad.*' A broken bottle can do a lot of damage to human flesh in a

48

very short time, but he had survived somehow to tell his story.

For years she had no conscious memory of picking up the bottle, of smashing it against the wooden dining table. Of lunging forward to attack, of reaching her target, of slicing through flesh, again and again until her Mother's piercing scream and clawing fingers had broken through something in her and she had stopped and looked at what she had done. She had never seen so much blood, was all she could remember thinking before she collapsed, falling across her Father's legs. She hoped she'd finished him off, but she hadn't. He was a survivor.

Her Mother retreated from life after that to hide in a one-room flat barely bigger than her daughter's cell. With her philosophy unable to rise to this last challenge, her willpower broken, she didn't want to know anything anymore. Her curtains and windows now remained closed. She made the trip to Milldale now and again, then stopped altogether, then even the letters stopped arriving. Except for one short note in the final year of her sentence. 'Your Father's dead. May he be at peace at last.' That was it. She noted that 'Father' had a capital 'F.' She hadn't replied.

*****

Rudi brings her toast and tea on a tray with home-made muesli and yoghurt for himself. "I should visit Mother." She loves the way he's never surprised by anything she says.

"Yeh, why not eh? She doesn't know she's gonna be a Granny does she?"

"I don't see how she could. I wonder if she'll be happy about it."

"Well you'll find out won't you?" She leans towards him and wipes a blob of yoghurt from his beard. He leans down, pulls up her T-shirt and kisses the taut skin of her belly. "Wouldn't it be good if she was really pleased and we could put all that behind us.'" She says.

"Suggest it to her. Make a new start with the arrival of a new life." *'Whatever happened yesterday is past. Today is new, a new start, a new life.'* Her Mother's voice echoes somewhere in her mind.

"Yeh maybe. Anyway we should go, she has a right to know."

"I don't think she stopped writing on purpose you know. I just don't think she could take it anymore."

"I hope you're right Rudi."

"I'm always right, you know that." She smiles across at him.

"Open the curtains will you. I want to see the Bluff this morning in sunlight. It helps me to stay strong." He pulls back the heavy fabric. The morning is clear, the outline of the mountain's weathered face is clean against the morning sky. Someone like Rudi, she thinks, has the power to change lives and he doesn't even know it.

Fork Tongued Frescoes

Cassie invited me in one day to see her 'pride and joy.' I didn't know what to expect. A waft of incense met me when she opened the front door but I wasn't prepared for what I saw then. They were everywhere. "Rosa says she doesn't mind what I paint on the walls. That was one reason I took the place. Won't live in a place where I can't paint the walls. You know what I mean?" I nodded.

From the brilliant light of an Australian summer morning I followed her into the gloomy hallway of her rented cottage. The walls, doors and ceilings of the little place were covered with a mass of serpents. Each coiling spiral of colour had yellow eyes except for the one Cassie was pointing to. "Me, see she's got green eyes, like me and she's red and gold, my favourite colours. She's mine. Do you like her?" I was unsure what to say, confronted with a vista of colourful snakes on my neighbour's house walls. It wasn't an experience I was familiar with. I struggled to answer. "She's beautiful, yes, did you paint them all?"

"Every single one honey. Idle hands do the devil's work so I'm busy every day. There's just no end to what my imagination comes up with. Some are based on real snakes, the rest just pure fantasy."

She swept her arms around indicating the extent of her artwork.

"I call them my fork-tongued frescoes." She giggled. I wanted some fresh air.

"I haven't seen the backyard since Mrs Carter lived here. Can we have a quick look?"

"Sure, you won't notice much difference. I'm not big on gardening. My babies don't give me much free time and I don't want them slithering out into the grass and disappearing." She laughed and moved her body in a belly-dancing type motion as she led me down the hallway.

Arranged on the paved patio were a few bedraggled-looking outdoor chairs grouped around a grubby table. "Take a seat, I'll get us some refreshment." She didn't ask what I wanted and soon returned with two glasses of some sort of fizzy drink. "Home-made ginger ale." She was smiling as I took my first sip. The bitter tang was a surprise.

"Mmm, unusual."

"Yeh, Gran's secret recipe. Has a special ingredient in it that gives it that extra bite." She smiled at her own pun. "Irish, she was, never got over St Patrick getting rid of all the snakey creatures from her beloved country, well that's the story anyway." She chuckled and gulped the rest of her drink.

"Tried to stop the pagan Celtic practices going on there but Gran reckoned it'd take more than St Patrick to do that. They carried on anyway. She'd know, she was pretty wild my Gran. Kept a snake in a tank in her kitchen. Felt like a kindred spirit to me. Loved them ever since."

"But Cassie, painting them on the walls is pretty weird, don't you think?"

"'Spose some people might think so." She was leaning forward and gesturing with her hands as she spoke.

"But for me it's everything. It's, how shall I say it, the outpouring of my inner self, my soul." She looked down and her previously animated face suddenly stilled. "Jim hates them. Hates me liking snakes and especially hates me painting them but he's got no idea how much they mean to me. No idea." Poor Jim I thought, probably creeps him out having his wife paint snakes all over the walls of his house.

"You're pretty serious about them aren't you Cassie?" I asked, not really knowing what else to say.

"Yes, I am." She looked at me again and smiled. "Each one of them is an aspect of me, so it's my life painted on those walls? You understand that don't you?" I nodded.

Having finished my drink I had a strong urge to leave. I said I understood completely then made out I had to leave because I was waiting for a phone call. Back home I felt somehow unsettled by the whole thing but I wasn't quite sure why. Sure it was unusual to paint snakes on your walls but eccentricity had always intrigued me.

It's strange how curiosity seduces. I saw her regularly after that. Neither Cassie nor I had jobs so we'd meet for coffee or a ginger ale or a cold beer but she'd always take me down the side path next to the house. She never invited me inside the house again but she'd talk about her passion as we sat on the patio surrounded by paintbrushes and rags.

"Jim doesn't understand me you know, thinks I'm crazy, but I'm not. You know I'm not, I'm painting the bedroom now." She winked in a knowing sort of way. It was funny how Cassie assumed I understood her, though I really knew very little about her. I'd asked a few questions about her past but she was a skillful evader.

Jim left for work early weekday mornings and arrived home late. Cassie had told me what he did but I couldn't remember exactly, something to do with marketing. They seemed like an odd match somehow. He was always dressed smartly, even on weekends yet Cassie dressed like she was reliving the hippie days of the seventies. Long skirts, gypsy blouses, wild jewellry, the works. Whenever I waved to Jim he only ever said 'Hi,' and carried on with whatever he was doing in the garden as if he didn't want to get to know me. I couldn't help wondering how he coped, especially at night, since Cassie had painted the bedroom. Poor guy, must have nightmares.

*****

One Saturday evening just as the light was fading I heard them next door. Cassie was screaming that she would not stop and Jim was shouting that she must, that he couldn't take it anymore. I was surprised to hear Jim shouting like this, he seemed such a quiet guy. Maybe he was one of those who bottled stuff up and then... Doors were slamming and I could hear both of them charging through the house. Jim stormed out, got into the car, revved it loudly and screeched out of the driveway. The house lights were on all night and I guessed that Cassie was in a wild painting frenzy and that by morning there would be lots more snakes. Angry, dangerous snakes.

Jim came back at noon the next day about half an hour after Cassie had gone out somewhere. I don't usually do this but I peeped out of the lounge window from behind the curtain to see what he was doing. He was carrying several large paint tins and brushes into the house. I could smell the paint. I guessed what he was doing. Cassie came home at three. Then screaming, swearing, smashing and door banging lasted for at least half an hour. Then silence.

By early evening there was still no sound. I didn't know what to do but the silence was unnerving. I couldn't settle so I thought I'd go and see if they were OK before dark set in.

I walked down the side lane to the back patio where Jim had left the empty paint tins stacked neatly against the walls. The back door was closed so I pushed it open. The paint fumes were overpowering. I looked down the hallway and I could see Jim lying on the groundsheet that was covering the floor. White paint was spilled and splattered all around him. My eyes took a moment to adjust to the sight - the walls, doors and ceiling were blank sheets of stark white, every snake obliterated except for the red and gold one with green eyes. Cassie's favourite, high up on the wall above where Jim was lying.

He was lying on his front and he looked odd. His head was skewed and I could see two tiny puncture marks on his neck and a thin trail of blood that had trickled and dried on his skin. I didn't touch him. I just stood and looked at his frozen face. His eyes were still open. Dizzy from paint fumes and shock I needed air. As I ran to the back door I could hear myself screaming out to Cassie. I couldn't stop myself even though I knew she couldn't hear my voice. I knew in that moment that I would never see Cassie again.

On the patio table was the jug of ginger ale and a glass. I don't know why now but I seized the jug and hurled it across the yard watching the liquid fly and waiting for the glass to smash into a shower of shards. Then I saw it. The slightest quiver of the blades of a patch of tall, thick unmown grass. Like there was a snake slithering along there at ground level.

First Published, *Hecate* Magazine.

Butterfly

She had felt obliged to move back in with Mother after Father died. Mother was lonely. Kate was single. It would benefit them both. That's what everyone said. It didn't bother Kate one way or the other.

Five to ten. Kate checked herself in the mirror. She eschewed make up and her hair was cut short to avoid having to 'mess about with it.' She was fussy about grooming though, her plain white blouses were washed and ironed to perfection and as soon as a hint of greyness appeared or the smallest stain they went into the charity shop box. Her tights were never laddered and her flat shoes always polished.

At ten twenty seven she let herself into *Vernon Smart's Photographic Studio* ready for a ten thirty start. Three minutes to organise her materials and check the list of jobs he wanted doing today.

Kate had never 'had a man' as Mother put it. Vernon was the closest she had ever been to anyone apart from Mother. She dusted his furniture, cleaned his floors and made his bed. She knew what he had for breakfast and that he never ate his crusts, that he liked lime marmalade and flannelette sheets and black underpants. He used unscented deodorant and clipped his nails every Tuesday. He was left handed and going bald.

She thought Vernon was beautiful, not handsome, beautiful - lean, muscular with an interesting angular face accentuated by his receding hairline. He moved like the world belonged to him and nothing frightened him, not that she knew about anyway.

At night Vernon was with her in her disturbing, sometimes shocking dreams that she tried to forget. How could a woman who'd never had a man imagine such things? She hoped she never spoke during her sleep with Mother in the next room.

*****

He'd scribbled on the back of a car park docket.

Hi Kate,

Hope you had a good weekend. Just the usual and help yourself to the cake in the fridge, Sybilla made it, I think she's trying to fatten me up. Oh and could you tidy up the costume cupboard, it's got a bit out of hand. Cheers, V.

This would be added to the collection of Vernon's notes stored in a box at the back of Kate's wardrobe.

After finishing most of her tasks, Kate had a small slice of the black forest cake for morning tea. It was the sort of cake Sybilla would make. Very little cake, mostly cream, cherries in some sort of liquor and curls of rich dark chocolate. 'Decadent' Sybilla would have called it. Last time Sybilla stayed at Vernon's she'd made a cake shaped like a breast with a cherry nipple in the centre.

The usual tasks didn't take long so after morning tea there was only the costume cupboard to tidy before going. Kate surveyed the dresses falling off hangers and piled on the floor as if an assortment of women had just stepped out of them. As she was hanging them back up she noticed something at the end of the rack. A green shiny bodysuit, the type that dancers wear. Attached to the wrists and the back was lace fabric falling into folds. This fabric was pale and very fine and covered in embroidery and fine beading. She lifted up the cuff of one sleeve, allowing a wing to unfold. It was like something from *A Midsummer Night's Dream* - as delicate as a dragonfly wing with veins embroidered in silver thread. Attached to the hanger was a green velvet eye mask, decorated with tiny coloured jewels and gold beads.

Kate walked over to Vernon's tiny bathroom with the costume. After locking the door, even though she was alone in the apartment, she undressed and pulled on the bodysuit taking great care of the wings. It fitted well. Looking down at the low neckline she saw the top of her bra showing. Gently lowering the top of the costume from her shoulders she took her bra off. The top was now tight over her full unsupported breasts. She was feeling hot and she hoped she wouldn't start sweating and make the costume damp or marked.

She unlocked the bathroom door and walked barefoot over to the mirror on tip toes to be as quiet as possible, like a guilty little girl. She allowed herself to look in the full length mirror, firstly gazing into her own eyes, then slowly daring herself to look further. The shiny bodysuit showed every curve of her body. The low neck revealed a cleavage she'd never wanted to notice. She looked alarmingly sexy.

She went back to the bathroom and retrieved the glorious mask. Putting it on as she returned to the mirror, relief was immediate. Her breathing slowed. She looked magnificent - whoever she was.

*****

Vernon opened the door. He smiled but didn't seem at all surprised to find Kate in full butterfly costume. "Don't tell me. Wow, you look fabulous babe."

"I'm sorry I…"

"Don't apologise honey, they're there to have fun with."

"I don't know what to say."

"I said it's OK, don't get so uptight. Dying for a coffee, want one?"

"Oh no please."

"Come on I'll make you a coffee. Just sit down." Kate wanted to get her clothes and leave and never return, never see Vernon again. She was unbearably aware that she was standing in a very tight, very sexy butterfly suit in front of her employer.

"I'll just change, OK."

"If you must, I was just going to suggest you stay in the costume and we do a few shots for fun. You look great you know. What do you think?"

"No, please."

"Come on Kate, look you've been working for me for three years. I trust you. You were just having a bit of fun, right. Come on, drink up and we'll do a few shots." Vernon was bringing the coffees over with a couple of huge slices of black forest. "Great cake, did you have some, it didn't look like it."

"Oh I just had a taste." Vernon leaned down to his plate and licked his slice of cake. "Mmm, delectable, got to eat it before the cream goes off."

"Look please, let me say, I do feel very bad about this. You trust me to be here and I go trying on your costumes. I don't feel right about it."

"And I said stop worrying. Kate, what is wrong with you? Loosen up darl. Here eat your cake." Kate looked at the enormous slice of rich cake as Vernon launched into his like he hadn't eaten for weeks.

"I'll just check the camera and we're off." Kate ate a few forkfuls of cake and got up.

"OK over here that's right. Now relax, forget I'm here, I know that's difficult so my models tell me, but just try it. Let yourself go. Hang on, you need a bit of lippie otherwise you're gonna look like a ghost when they come out. Have you got some?"

"No I don't wear it to work."

"OK look I've got some of Sybs here. I'll wipe the top so it's clean. Here go over to the mirror and do your stuff." He handed her a dark red lipstick. When she'd put it on it made her lips look like she'd eaten a bowl of crushed raspberries.

"Now stand here and do just what I tell you. I'll take quite a few and then you can have a look at them and see what you think." He took his place behind the camera. Kate felt like she was naked. "Kate, loosen up. Tell you what. Close your eyes so you can't see me and just relax and pose. Do what you like. Have some fun. No-one'll recognise you in that costume so you've got nothing to worry about. You look fantastic. Most women'd die for a figure like yours."

61

She felt very hot and something else she wasn't sure of. No one can recognise me she thought. She heard the camera clicking. She kept her eyes closed.

"Great Kate, you look fantastic darling. You're a natural. Now do your stuff just relax into it. Make the most of it. You're a beautiful woman. Where have you been hiding? That's it, smile, gorgeous. Yeh, great, hold that." His admiration washed over her like a warm bath. She smiled, she pouted, she laughed, she flirted.

"You're wonderful Kate. Keep going. Come on." She wrapped the gorgeous wings around her. "OK now how about without the mask. Let's see that face."

Kate ripped off the mask, opened her eyes and met Vernon's. He was smiling at her. She looked away. Her stomach seized. She felt a burning sensation rising up her neck.

"That's enough. I really need to go…please." She hurried towards the bathroom. As she passed Vernon he gently took hold of her arm.

"Kate, please, don't be upset. What's wrong. It's just fun. I know it's nerve racking when you haven't been photographed before but you're so good. Please." She could feel him trying to make eye contact with her but she wouldn't look up.

"I can't explain. Please let me go Vernon." She hadn't called him by his name before, never feeling quite confident enough to be so intimate.

In the bathroom she grabbed the edge of the basin and stared into the mirror. She ran the water and scrubbed her lips roughly with soap to rid herself of the lipstick. She peeled off the butterfly, folded it up on the chair and dressed as hot tears ran down her face. She splashed her face with cold water, breathed deeply and looked at herself in her own clothes. She opened the door. Vernon was fiddling with his camera. Not looking at him she marched across the room. "I have to go now, thank you for taking the photographs." Vernon said nothing and didn't look up.

Outside in the fresh air she felt less choked. Catching the bus and sitting with other people helped her. She tried not to think, to just focus on looking out of the window at everyday life. She wanted to get into her bed and have a sleep.

*****

"That you Kate?"

"Yes Mum."

"I've just made a pot."

"OK just let me get my coat off and I'll be with you." She closed her bedroom door and lay on her bed. The images rushed into her head as soon as she was lying down. Standing in front of Vernon pouting with thick dark red lips, her lean body in a green shiny costume with a plunging neckline. Her cheeks burned at the memory and her body felt strangely agitated.

She grabbed a pen and wrote a short note saying she could no longer work for him 'for family reasons,' finishing with a request that he not ring her. She put it in her handbag to post later that day when she would make an excuse to go out again. Feeling more composed now the letter was written she brushed her hair and joined Mother in the kitchen.

*****

He didn't ring. She knew he wouldn't. She had asked him not to ring. He was man of his word. A man of honour. She had allowed herself to be vulnerable and he had respected her, but she couldn't face him now or ever again. "Look here love, here's a job you might want to go for. 'Cleaner wanted for elderly lady one day a week.' That would replace the photographer. Pity he had to go overseas. Still they all do those types, always off somewhere or other. Here have a look." Kate took the local paper from Mother and read the ad. "Sounds good Mum. If you've finished I'll just have a look through."

Mother left the table and sat in the lounge in her favourite armchair with her feet up on an old velvet covered footstool. "Another cup'd be nice love, when you're ready, no rush." She looked so comfortable there in Kate's lounge room. So at home. For a moment Kate wondered how Vernon would respond to Mother. He would be charming of course. And Mother? Mother would giggle like a schoolgirl as Vernon flirted with her. That was until she felt she knew him a little then the questions would start. But what if Mother wasn't there? How would she, Kate, respond if Vernon was in her lounge room without Mother there? "I'll have one of those chocolate crunch fingers too love, but as I said no rush." What if she was free to have anyone she liked in her home, anyone, anytime. She'd never thought about that before now. "OK, coming, won't be a minute."

First Published, *New England Review*.

Jesse

"What the hell are you doing here? Answer me. No? Go on then, get outa here." He edges past her staring down at his oversized feet. Shards of silence splice him open. She knows who he is. Only a few more steps. Run. Like that other time, he ran too, down to the beach into the freezing black surf. This time though, he runs home.

"You right Jess? You look buggered mate."

"Need some sleep that's all.' He escapes to his room feigning gut ache. He gets out the news article he keeps folded up at the back of his bookcase. '*Outrage: Thugs Desecrate Baby's Grave.*' Thugs. Hour upon hour he tosses in the sheets. Her face stares at him from inside his head, a little dead baby in her arms.

He gets up before dawn, knowing what he needs to do. He walks slowly, stepping over creaky boards. He hears his family's sleep sounds. There's his Mum's flowery notepaper on the kitchen shelf next to the jug that Grandma gave her last Christmas. His jelly hand holds the pen and he writes:

> *I was at your baby's grave the other day. I go there lots but it don't help.*
>
> *I wish I could go back in time because if I could I wouldn't do it this time. When they were dancing round with the flowers out of your baby's vase in their hair and then they broke the vase I felt real*

bad. I told them to stop but they were too out of it.
I read your baby's name. It's the same as mine.

I'm really sorry REALLY REALLY sorry. I'm a
real shit.

Jesse Sims

The longest letter he's ever written. There's an envelope left over from one of his sister's birthday cards. He crosses out '*To Courtney*'.

He arrives early. It's freezing and dew damp. Someone's arranged fresh roses in the vase on the tiny grave. There's a baby in a little wooden box under that soil he thinks. He feels even colder than when he left home. He stares at the ugly white 'N' that Nathan scratched that night with a shard of smashed beer bottle. Then Nathan had anointed the headstone with his steaming urine, joking about how he could piss hot beer.

He leans the envelope against the vase, making sure it's straight. Then he leaves. The crunching of the gravel under his trainers sounds so loud he wants to tiptoe instead but that's too slow. He keeps running, following his clouds of white breath and listening to his own gasping.

Next morning he's back again. The envelope's still there. She hasn't been. Looking closer to check it hadn't got too damp he sees it isn't his envelope. It's blank where he had scribbled out Courtney's name. Leaning forward so as not to step on the grave he picks it up. Something inside him doesn't want to open it and something else does.

Quivering, his fingers pull out the turquoise paper, her writing's small and neat.

I appreciate your letter. At least one of you has the balls to say sorry.

I can't begin to understand you and I know you've no idea what this has done to me. I'm not going to tell you my Jesse's story because that would betray him. He was the best thing in my life and he was taken away from me and you and your friends made fun of that.

If you ever become a father and have a little baby you'll realise what you've done, what was a stupid bit of sick fun for you was the meanest, vilest thing anyone's ever done to me. May God help you.

There was no signature.

His dreams are worse. He wakes in tears, shaking, hoping he hasn't cried out in his sleep. His Mum's really annoying him, asking about his early morning walks and why he doesn't look well. He pushes her away when she tries to hug him. "What's wrong with you Jess, something's up. Come on love what is it?"

"Leave me alone will you, you're always poking your nose into my life." He stalks out of the house and stays out all day but he doesn't see his mates. He hangs around the oval and the mall. He stays out till late sitting in McDonalds staring at the chicks laughing and joking. He knows his Mum's worrying but why can't she just chill and leave him alone? Courtney's hassling him too, asking him whether he's taking drugs or what, "Mum's really worried about you, it's not fair, what's up?"

Arriving early the next day, he crouches, out of sight, next to the caretaker's shed. She comes every day but he's not sure what time. The waiting's getting unbearable. He's so tense he's busting to punch something - hard. He sees her approaching and he's suddenly desperate to go to the toilet and clutches himself like a child. She kneels near the vase. He creeps forward, hoping he won't wet himself. He doesn't want to scare her so he calls out from a little way off. "Hey, please, I wanna talk to you." She looks around, trying to work out where the voice came from. Then she sees him. "Who are you? Oh, the one from the other day." She's frowning. Her fine fair hair's blowing in the breeze and sticking to her face and she keeps moving it away. "I wrote the letter," he blurts. She turns her face away from him as if he makes her feel sick.

"Please, I'm really sorry, honest. I can't sleep, please."

"Stop it!" She turns and stares straight into his eyes. Her face is mist pale and too young to be so lined, her mouth's tight but her eyes are on fire. "Go away and don't write to me or come here ever again. The way you can feel better is by staying away. Do you hear me?"

"Please." He's crying now and pleading. "Just say you don't hate me. I can't stand it. Please, I don't know what to do. I feel so…" He can't say any more. She sees a skinny boy, in oversized shorts with a wet, red face and his hands between his legs. "Listen, how bad you feel, that you can't stand it, that you can't sleep. That's how it is for me all the time, every day, every minute, right. Get it?" She's shouting and starting to cry. "I thought I couldn't stand it either. I thought it couldn't get any worse after Jesse died, but it did, you and your friends made sure of that. But I do stand it. I have to. So you can stand it too. At least you've faced it, which is more than those other cowards you call mates have. If you're really sorry you'll stand up to them. You'll tell them what you think of them. You'll tell them you're not one of them anymore. If you've got the guts, which I doubt. Now get out of here, get a life and stay out of mine."

Tears wind down her face and drip off her chin. She turns away as he leaves.

Outside the cemetery he stops behind a tree. He's peeing and sobbing at the same time. Then he runs as fast as he can. Thank God no-one's home. He spews in the toilet, then falls on his bed and sleeps. In his dream he's standing near the grave, wetting himself. A stain spreads across his shorts, runs down his legs into a pool at his feet. His mates are laughing and she's there watching with those flaming eyes, waiting to see if he's brave enough. He wakes up in a full sweat, showers and gets dressed in clean clothes.

Striding across the park he sees them there, huddled around the fountain, with bottles in brown paper bags, laughing and cursing. Tins, fast food wrappers and cigarette butts litter the ground. Moving closer, he's breathing faster and his heart's racing but he's not nervous – oh no, he's powering, never felt so sure of himself in his life. "Hey matey you look like you're up to somethin'," calls Nathan. Jesse doesn't smile. He knows his voice will be strong and clear. "I've got some news for you lot that you're not gonna wanna hear."

"Don't tell us then." Someone laughs. Someone else farts.

"Oh no, I'm gonna tell you." Jesse stares into the eyes of each group member in turn. He can't recall later exactly what happens then, he just remembers that they all stop laughing and talking. They stand very still and some of them look worried. Jesse isn't scared though, he feels stronger than he's ever felt in his whole life, he's never felt anything like this ever before, as if he can say anything, do anything, be anything. He feels unstoppable...

Drinking With Jesus

Penelope at the welfare hears my story every week. She gives me tea and carrot cake with too much icing and she listens. She doesn't do much else but maybe that's enough. There's a picture of Jesus on the wall above her desk - the only picture in the room. I always end up sitting opposite Jesus so he and I spend the session trying to avoid each other. Well I try to avoid him anyway. Something about those brown eyes and that beard and long hair remind me of Jed and I don't want to be reminded of Jed. I'll ask her if I can sit in a different place. I could ask her to take the picture down I suppose but I'd feel uncomfortable - I mean, it is a church welfare service.

Next week though I'll ask her if I can move so I'm not facing him. Then she'll start asking questions about why I can't face Jesus. That's the trouble, they want to know everything and they seem to have ways of finding out. I suppose that's what they're paid for, unless she isn't paid because it's a church place. I don't know, never thought of that.

*****

"Does Jesus bother you Jim?"

"Not bother, it's just that it's like he's staring down at me."

"And how does that feel for you?"

"Don't like it much, makes me jittery."

"Jittery?"

"Yeh, sort of, I just feel odd that's all."

"Have you felt like this at other times?"

"'Spose, whenever somebody's staring down at me."

"Mmm staring *down,* so it has something to do with Jesus being above you?" She went on with that line for a while and it led back to my Father of course. Looking down at me. Obvious of course. Easy too, when he was so tall.

Everyone knows that counsellors get you talking about your childhood. We dug up - well in a manner of speaking - the family, school, the footy team, where Annie and I met when we were fourteen. All that stuff. It was hard, going back over it all. How we met, how we fell in love and got married on her 18th birthday. I don't know now that we did fall in love but whatever we did fall into it was nice at the time. I remember Jed asking me if it was love or just lust? He said he knew what real love was.

*****

I remember that night on my way home from work. At the time I thought it was a coincidence but now, come to think of it, you must've worked out that I left the warehouse at five so I'd get to Mason's Corner at ten past. You were waiting for me. I got off the bus and there you were at the stop.

You were wearing a grey woolly hat pulled down over your ears and your hair was sticking out the bottom. It would've looked funny on anyone else but you never looked funny. You had your hands in your jacket pockets and you were hunched over against the wind. You didn't say hello or anything you just looked down at me. I was so scared of you mate. I mean you are one tall, scary bastard. I know what you were thinking Jed. I could feel it when you looked down at me that night. I know why she felt so safe with you. Anyone'd feel safe with you on their side. Tall and tough but with a face like Jesus. That, Jed, is what Annie said about you the night after Bazza's party. 'A face like Jesus.' Her expression'd changed and her eyes seemed to be looking at something that wasn't there.

So you took her Jed. You took her from me. Oh, you'll say she went of her own choosing. That she was an adult who made a free choice. You'll say it was over between us anyway. But the truth is you took her. There was no stopping it. It was just one of those things. Maybe if Annie and I hadn't met so young, the light wouldn't have gone out in our marriage. But it had. It had been out for ages. We were living in the dark. And there you were. Jed with a face like Jesus, a shining light. I don't blame her. But you. You knew what you were doing. You could see how she was that night. You could've put her off. But no, you just went right ahead, enjoying every minute of it. I know I had my problems - it was a weakness. Penelope says it's a disease that runs in families.

*****

When I'm finished at the church I go down the club for lunch. Brian's always waiting for me. Brian's a good mate, always has been. We queue up at the bistro and have a good feed for a few dollars. Roast, vegs, gravy, then apple pie and ice cream. Brian and I have been drinking mates for ten years now. I only have orange juice now of course. He doesn't understand why I go and see Penelope. He says all I need is a good mate like him to keep me on the straight and narrow. But it's OK for Brian. He likes living on his own. I don't.

Without Brian I don't think I'd have got through Annie going. After she left I wasn't in real good shape. For a long while I'd wake up and it'd take ages before I realized she wasn't in the bed. I'd be sure she was there. I'd even speak to her sometimes, then when I opened my eyes I'd realize that I was in bed on my own. It would all come back and I'd lie there and not want to ever get out of bed - sometimes I'd lie there all day. No one ever knew that, not even Brian. Other days I'd get up and not get dressed and just get out the whiskey and drink till I couldn't think.

After about two months things were getting quite bad. I wasn't mowing the grass or putting the bin out and stuff was piling up outside. Some interfering bugger in the street must've rung the church and Penelope came round. She seemed nice and said she was just calling by to see how I was doing. Next thing I know I'd agreed to go and see her at the church because I'd told her about my drinking and about Annie.

*****

"Jim." Penelope was leaning over the desk, frowning.
"Yeh."

"I'd like to talk about jealousy and what it does to people."

"Waste of bloody time."

"What do you mean?"

"Been through that. It's useless, makes you sick, it can drive you mad you know."

"But it didn't drive you mad Jim?"

"I dealt with it."

"How did you deal with it Jim?"

"You just have to deal with it. Life goes on. What's the point? She'd been wanting to go for years, it was just a case of the right guy coming along at the right time and along came Jesus Jed and…."

"And what Jim?"

"Do you know something I would've killed that bastard if I hadn't been such a coward but that's my problem. I'm a coward. If I'd had the balls to kill Jesus she might have loved me again."

"Jim, if you'd killed Jed you'd be in jail. But I know what you're saying."

"Yeh, I think you do too."

*****

I go home. I read the *Telegraph* from cover to cover. I watch a few dumb TV shows. I have a pie for tea. Then I get out my Bible. The Gospels. The story of Jesus. Jesus wasn't a coward. Jesus was one brave man and he suffered. Did he suffer. We all have our cross to bear Mum used to say. Yeh, tell me about it. I look at the scrawly writing in the front. '*To Jim, Take this with you through life son and remember to forgive. All my love, Mum.*' Ha! Forgiveness.

Mum forgave the drunk who fathered me too many times and look where it got her. I don't agree with you Mum, sorry. Thanks for the thought but I don't want to forgive. Fester. That's what she used to call it. '*Your anger will fester in your heart.*' She'd say. '*And it'll kill you. When you forgive, your heart can be free.*' Her heart might've been free but she was still a prisoner in her own life. My Father was the jailer. I won't forgive. I want to fester. I don't want to be free. What's the point? Free to do what? Murder Jed with my own bare hands?

It's getting close to Christmas. It's funny, round Christmas, some people get happier and some get real cranky. And suddenly Jesus is everywhere. It's like he hides all year and then out he comes at Christmas for an annual performance. Brian thinks Christmas is a waste of money but I tell him not to be so bloody miserable.

Christmas Eve I checked my post box as usual expecting a few ads but there was an envelope in there. I could see it was a card through the thin envelope. Haven't had a Christmas card for years. Used to get one from Mum. God rest her soul. Has Penelope sent me a card? When I opened it I was so shocked I couldn't move. '*To Jim, Merry Christmas, Annie.*' That was it. No letter. Just that. I thought it was a nasty joke. I put it in a drawer. Couldn't throw it out. Just in case. Tried not to think about it. Didn't even tell Brian when we had Christmas dinner at the Club.

A week later another one arrived. '*To Jim, Happy New Year, Annie.*' The photo inside gave me a turn. There we were, the two of us, that day at the zoo. I sat and studied that photo for a very long time. Must've been forty years ago. Annie had long hair and I've got my arm round her. Who the hell is sending these? I almost had a drink that day looking at that photo. But I didn't. I had to stay strong.

*****

"So Jim what do you make of it?" Penelope looks a bit plumper than before Christmas and a bit tireder - too much celebrating maybe."

"Dunno, doesn't make any sense to me. Gives me the creeps." I'd decided to tell her, nothing to lose really.

"In what way?" She looked at the photo.

"That someone's got that photo of us and they don't say who they are."

"So you don't think it's Annie?"

"She wouldn't."

"You sure of that?" What a question. She looked at me over her reading glasses.

"'Course not, I need to go." I reached across to grab the photo. I shouldn't have I know but she was annoying me. It was still between her fingers and it ripped right in two. She gasped and put her hand to her mouth.

"Jim, oh no, I'm sorry, it wasn't your fault. Look let's stick it together." She was acting panicky and rummaging in her top drawer. I picked up the two pieces of photo and walked out.

Six months now and I haven't been back to the welfare. Penelope wrote to me a couple of times. She went on about wanting to 're-establish contact' but I think I'm better off without it. The letters have been coming every so often but no more photos. I say letters but what I really mean is notes. They never have more than about five words to them and they're always signed '*Annie.*' I've pinned them all to the wall above the kitchen table. Stupid really, it's probably some nutter from the Club whose been listening to me and Brian talking.

Don't see Brian much now because he's in and out of hospital and I can't get there to see him. It gets pretty quiet here on my own so I did something last week I never thought I'd ever do. I bought myself a picture of Jesus. I was walking past the Catholic shop one day and I noticed this picture. It was something about the eyes of this Jesus that looked really kind.

I went inside. I'd never been in before. It was one of those musty op shops with clothes racks and shelves of odd cups and bowls. I asked the old lady behind the counter the price of the Jesus picture and she said I could have it for 50c because it'd been in the window for ages. Funny I thought, I go past this shop all the time and I'd never noticed it before. She wrapped the picture in a crumpled plastic bag and said it must've been waiting just for me to buy it and God bless me.

When I got the picture home I dusted it and looked around the for a good place to hang it. In the end I stood it on my kitchen table. When I eat he's there with me. This picture doesn't bother me like the one at the welfare used to. Maybe it's because I chose it myself or maybe because he's not looking down at me. Whenever I sit at the table I start to talk to him. I tell him what I've been thinking and doing - which isn't much. He has such a kind face that it feels like he's listening to me and sometimes I get ideas after I've talked to him and what's funny is that I've told him a whole lot more than I ever told Penelope and even Brian come to think of it.

*****

I've got used to them coming now. In fact I look forward to them. Always the same size envelope, always just a few words *'Hope you're well,'* or *'Have a good week,'* that sort of thing so I was expecting the same sort of thing this time but instead it said: *'I'm coming to see you tomorrow, Annie.'* That was it. I can't remember feeling so shocked since the day she told me about Jed. It took all my strength to open the cabinet and pour myself a whiskey, I felt like my bones had turned to jelly. Hadn't touched a drop since she left. It's been a hell of a hard battle but I thought if I could beat it she might come back. She didn't. I sat for a long time with that whiskey looking at the note. I don't know how long I sat there but it had got dark and I felt dog tired.

I couldn't sleep and ended up with the whiskey bottle on the kitchen table talking to Jesus. If I talked out loud it seemed to block out everything so I told Jesus the story of my life. When the whiskey bottle was empty I still wasn't asleep so I moved to the bedroom and fell onto my mattress. I must've been asleep for ages because it was light and I could hear knocking. I thought it must be the throbbing inside my head. I pulled myself up and listened. It was the front door. That's right, she said she was coming today. I patted down my hair, stuffed a mint in my mouth and tried to hurry to the door even though I couldn't see straight with the pain in my head.

At first I wasn't sure if they were real or not. He was bent over so not as tall. She had her arm through his. All I could think about was how old they looked and I realized I must look the same to them. It's a shock when you haven't seen someone for years. You expect them to look the same as last time and they don't. Annie still had those bright, brown eyes but her thick brown hair was now grey and she looked shorter than I remembered. Jed was thinner and he wasn't scary any more. He looked more like some grandad with untidy grey hair and a bit of a beard.

"Jim." That was all she said. I didn't answer.

"Can we come in Jim?" Annie said and I remember I still didn't answer, I just pulled the door open. They walked along the hall and into the kitchen. The empty whiskey bottle was still on the table like an exhibit in a court case. We all looked at it but no one said anything. I couldn't even start to explain how many years it was since I'd had a drink. Jed still hadn't spoken.

"Jim, we wanted to say goodbye. We're leaving the area. We sold our place and we've been staying with Luke and his family until our new place was available. It's up north where it's warmer. So unless you travel I don't think we'll get to see each other again. So I thought I owed it to you to come and say goodbye. Jed agreed, he said it was time to move

80

on, literally." All I could think about were all her handwritten notes pinned on the wall in front of us. I could see her looking at them.

"Sorry, I hope they didn't upset you. I just had to do it. Don't know why." Annie didn't seem to notice that Jed was there. "I wanted to see you Jim. Luke found your address for me."

"Can I get you anything?" I mumbled, I think I was in shock and I felt too tired to say anything else. She said they'd stay for a cup of tea. They sat together on the old leather sofa that the church gave me last year.

"That came from God so no misbehaving on it." I joked. I can't believe I said that now.

"Oh he's well past that." Annie joked back and Jed's expression didn't change. Her face was pretty lined but I could still make out the Annie that I knew. She was still a smiler. That'd been my nickname for her 'smiler.'

Jed sat still and silent and looked at a point on the floor in front of him. He'd got so much thinner that his clothes were loose on him. I couldn't believe I'd hated him so much. I didn't seem to feel that any more. "So you're a Christian now eh?" Annie said, pointing at Jesus. She didn't wait for my reply.

"I know lots of folks get religion at our age. A friend at the end eh." She laughed again. I didn't know how to explain what Jesus was doing there.

"Well, are you Christian these days?" She wasn't going to let me off.

"No not really Christian. I just find the picture helps.'" She pointed at Jed who still hadn't spoken.

"He used to remind me of Jesus when he was younger with his long brown hair and beard. Changed a bit hasn't he?" She was speaking again as if he wasn't there in the room.

"Don't we all?" I said. She moved closer to me, leaned towards the picture and spoke to Jesus.

"You take care of him now OK. He's a very special man is Jim." She turned her face to me and studied my face. "You're looking good."

"I try to look after myself."

"Life's about not repeating the mistakes of the past - isn't that right?" I could sense she wanted an answer.

"I guess that's part of it."

"I've made mistakes Jim."

"We all have Annie." She looked at her watch and turned and pulled at Jed's sleeve to get him to move.

"Luke's coming at three to pick us up." Jed hoisted himself up and she led him through the kitchen door and down the hall. They hadn't said one word to each other the whole time. I opened the front door to let them out. At the front gate she turned to me and said.

"Please try and forgive me Jim. Remember, Jesus teaches forgiveness." I couldn't think of anything to say at that last moment. The words seemed trapped somewhere inside my throat along with Mum's words about forgiveness.

"Oh, and I promise. No more notes. No need. I've seen you now." She guided Jed along the path. I saw Luke's car pull up. I didn't wait to see them get in. I closed the door, walked back to the lounge room and got out another bottle of whiskey. I sat down at the kitchen table. I thought of Jed's sunken face and grey hair as I looked into the eyes of the young man in the photograph. I poured myself a large glass and raised a toast to the young Jesus.

"To forgiveness." I said out loud with a laugh, clinked my glass against the picture frame, sculled the whiskey and poured myself another one.

Vertigo

Jackie built a cubby in the Banksia for Jiffy the cat, who wouldn't go in it of course. "Let's make it bigger." Jackie pulled me by the sleeve. I'd had enough of cubby building, handing Jackie pieces of timber and searching for nails in Dad's shed. But she was unstoppable, ferreting through the yard and Dad's woodpiles with no fear of spiders or snakes. "Pass me the hammer spoilsport." She yelled at me. When God gave out energy he gave so much to Jackie there wasn't much left over for me.

She hammered and I did whatever else to extend the cat cubby to human size. "Won't be fancy, just the two of us will fit." I would've been happy for Jackie to build a cubby just for herself and the cat but Jackie loved me so much she wanted me to be with her, to love what she loved. I did try very hard.

I told Jackie I needed to go to the toilet and wandered over to the house, kicking bits of dry gum bark and stones out of my way.   Mum and Dad were sitting on the verandah smoking. Dad rolled his own and would light one and pass it to Mum who would take a couple of puffs and hand it back to him. Dad had arranged the old cane chairs so that their wobbly legs straddled the missing planks. Sitting was safe as long as you kept still. Jackie was not allowed to sit in them because she couldn't be trusted to do that. "You'll be alright Laura. Just be a bit careful." Dad said. "Don't want the bookworm getting injured reading do we now?" Calling me 'bookworm' was an easy way out of having to understand a daughter who was so different to him, a gardener, a man who loved doing physical work until he was so tired he could hardly walk.

Mum thought I was lazy but I wasn't. I just didn't want to build cubbies. "Here love, take these sandwiches out to Jackie and see if you can do anything now to help her." I took the sandwiches over but I didn't offer to help. "Come up Laura. Share my sandwiches with me." I couldn't think of an excuse so I let Jackie help me up using the chunks of timber she'd nailed to the Banksia's rough trunk. She pulled me over to look at the neighbour's patch of ground littered with rusty bits of machines. I tried to sound excited. "Sit there, look I've made us a table." She pulled over an old crate and put a cloth on it, took the bag from me and spread the sandwiches out on a red plastic plate. Stuffing the soft bread into her mouth, Jackie talked with her mouth full about the adventures we were going to have. After we'd finished I said I needed to go. Jackie's smile dropped. "Come on you don't have to do anything. You can watch me. You can read if you like."

Jackie hated reading. She couldn't see how anyone could want to stay still looking at 'black squiggles.' I wondered sometimes if she had any imagination but I worked out that we just had different types of imagination. Jackie explored her imagination through movement, through doing. She would imagine she had superhuman powers by climbing up the drainpipe and onto our house roof. Her adventures took place as far above the ground as she could get herself. Now, high above our yard I needed some space from her world. "I'm a bit tired really." I said to her. I had more excuses for escaping than anyone had ever had. That would be my first book '*Laura's Escape Manual – how to get away from Anyone, Anytime, Anywhere*' by Laura Baldwin. "Get your book, bring it up here and sit with me. Oh go on, please."

*****

The idea came to me in a flash looking down on the Brown's Hill's Hoist and Mrs Brown's flapping undies. "Jackie it's very high up here. I don't like heights. I feel a bit sick. I need to go and lie down."

"You never minded heights before, you're making that up." Her voice was ringing in my ears. I wanted to scream, "Shut up can't you, just shut up!"

I saw myself grabbing her, holding my hand over her mouth. "I'm not making it up. Since the swing I don't like heights anymore." I looked at Jackie's broad tanned face and just at that moment, I didn't like my sister. I had to look away. I turned my back and walked across the wooden planks then I had to turn towards her to go down the steps.

She stood above me without smiling, her eyes watery. "Why can't you just stay up here with me for a few more minutes?" I didn't answer. "You're selfish you are." I started climbing down the steps. When I reached the ground I walked away while she shouted for me to come back up. For a moment I wished she would slip and fall, all the way to the ground, just like I had 'that day'.

We never talked about 'that day.' It hung over us like a dark cloud. Even on the brightest, sunniest morning, it would cast a tiny shadow across whatever we were doing. In an odd way though, it bound us to one another with the power that secrets have over people. Jackie and James Crown, the tallest boy in the school, had tied one end of a thick rope around the highest branch of an old gum that stood about two metres from the edge of a gully. They knotted the other end of the rope and bound lengths of old cotton sheet around the knot to form a lump big enough for someone to sit on and put the rope between their legs. Then the swinger would walk backwards, push, lift their feet and sail out way over the gully and back again. The branch was so high it allowed the swing to make a long slow arc over the gully to a high point where it would hang for a second, suspended over the terrifying drop, then glide backwards to safety.

On that day it was my turn to share in Jackie's excitement. She knew she should never have pushed me so hard as I left the ground but she desperately wanted me to feel her joy as I soared out over the gully. I said it didn't look safe. The old rope looked dangerously frayed and slimy with age but she wouldn't have it. It was fine, been there for years and wasn't going to break with a lightweight like me on it.

I should have stood my ground but she was bigger, louder, older. Of course she was right. The rope didn't break. I slipped instead. The sheer terror of feeling my hands lose their grip on that rope and my body lurch to the side returns sometimes. It was only because I missed the rocky outcrop and landed on a woody shrub at the bottom of the gully that I'm alive today. Luckily it was winter and I was wearing a padded jacket to soften my landing. I ended up on my back with a few cuts to my legs and arms from the branches.

I don't know how long I'd passed out for but it was long enough for Jackie to have climbed down the side of the gully to reach me. She shook me and cried out in a high pitched voice that didn't sound like hers at all. When I opened my eyes she broke into loud sobs and leaned over me and hugged me hard which hurt. She wailed something about thinking she'd killed me and that Mum and Dad would kill her when they found out. She gave me some water and a couple of toffees. I rolled out of the shrub as slowly as I could so I didn't hurt myself more. I remember standing up and feeling weak and shaky all over, I bent over and spewed all over the bush. The sick tasted vile so Jackie handed me some more lollies and water. Sick was all over the bush and dripping onto the ground and I started to cry to think I'd done that to the bush that had saved my life.

Jackie put her arm round me and said she knew a way back up to the top without climbing so we walked for about ten minutes till we came to an open grassy area which led us back towards home. We didn't pass the swing and we never went there or spoke of the accident again.

When we got nearly home Jackie stopped and told me to sit down. She sat really close, put her arm around my shoulder and leaned her head towards my face. She whispered, "Let's not tell Mum and Dad. They'll just be worried and you're OK aren't you?" I nodded and she kissed me on the cheek. "You won't ever tell them will you, promise?" I agreed and we made a blood pact that we'd never tell anyone. I had lots of little cuts and scratches on my arms so she just picked off a bit of dried blood to make one ooze again. She found a sharp stone and scratched herself hard so that it cut her skin and blood trickled out. Rubbing her cut against my scratch, she said some words she'd made up.

After that she asked me if I could act as if nothing was wrong so that Mum and Dad wouldn't be worried. I'd just say I'd fallen into a bush and got scratched. I realize now that the pact was to protect her from Mum and Dad. I only agreed because I was so shocked from my fall that I didn't have the energy to disagree. From that day on she was a different kind of sister. Somewhere in her brain there was an imprinted message that must have read. *'You didn't take care of your little sister, you nearly killed her. Next time you won't be so lucky.'*

After that day her love for me seemed to become the main focus of her life. She wanted me to be with her all the time and share everything she did. She wanted much more of me than I was able to give to her. She also changed in herself. She'd always been the tomboy, climbing trees and kicking balls. After that day instead of becoming more cautious, she took more and bigger risks, climbing trees she had thought too difficult and walking out along high branches balancing with her arms out like a tightrope walker. I wanted to shout at her to come down but I thought that she might lose her balance and fall and not be as lucky as I'd been. She would fall straight onto the hard baked earth of our backyard - in my mind I could hear the crack as her head hit the ground.

*****

Right now though, I'd escaped from her cubby house and sandwiches by pretending I was afraid of heights. I should have thought of it before but for some reason it just came to me then up there in the cubby. By the time I reached the toilet I really did feel queasy but not because of the height but because I realized that I'd wished Jackie would fall and it had brought back all those memories of 'that day'.

I knelt down next to the toilet bowl. My stomach was churning and a bit of sick rose into my mouth and burned my throat so I spat it into the water. The toilet smelt like a zoo. Suddenly I spewed up the sandwiches, coughing and spluttering as they landed in the toilet bowl. Grabbing some paper to wipe my mouth I heard Mum's voice. "Laura, you OK in there? I heard you being sick. Are you alright love?" I didn't answer but just sat, leaning my back against the wall. I could smell the sick because I hadn't flushed the toilet. It smelt just like when I was sick on the bush after the accident.

Mum left and came back with Dad and Jackie. Dad fiddled with the lock. After a while the door opened and the three of them were there. I didn't look at them. I didn't want to see their faces. Mum rushed in and pulled me up off the floor. "What's wrong, Laura? Why are you lying on the dirty floor?" She helped me up and led me out of the toilet. The other two didn't say anything. We walked to the bathroom and she washed my hands and face like I was little again. Then she put me to bed without undressing me and tucked me in.

*****

Next morning I felt very weak and I decided I would act as if nothing had happened yesterday. My family were at the table and my place was set. As usual, the four cereal boxes were on the bench with the milk and the sugar. "Morning love, how are you now?" I knew Mum would speak first. Dad and Jackie said nothing. I got some wheat flakes and milk and sat at the table. "You don't have to go in the cubby again. It's OK," said Jackie frowning as she spoke. Mum cleared her throat "We didn't realize that you don't like heights but now we do." I looked at them and said "I didn't really know either till yesterday." I felt bad lying to my family but I really didn't want to go up to the cubby anymore.

"Laura, I'm really, really sorry, I didn't know about you being frightened. So I've decided I'm going to build you and I the best cubby ever but it'll be on the ground so we can be together in it all the time and you won't be frightened. What do you think?" Mum and Dad were smiling. They'd solved my fear of heights problem but Jackie and I could still play together. I was cornered.

Mum and Dad didn't seem to notice how Jackie pushed me into playing with her. Come to think of it they didn't notice much of what we did. Out of sight, out of mind seemed to be their child-rearing philosophy. They were too busy with each other to notice much what their children were up to. Mum had us both before she was twenty - she wanted to get her child bearing over and done with quickly and get back to her real passion in life - Dad. I used to look at Jackie trying desperately to get their attention. I wondered why she wasted her time.

I wrote my first story on Jackie's tenth birthday when Mum forgot to buy her a present and wrapped up one she'd bought for Grandma and pretended it was for Jackie. We all knew she'd forgotten but Jackie pretended she loved the gift set of '*Old Roses*' soap and talcum powder.

*****

Jackie loved the house because the rambling style and the surrounding bush gave her freedom to run and climb and build and swing - anything her athletic body wanted to do. Jackie was a Blessington. In the photos Dad showed us were strong, tall men and women creating the Blessington story with their own physical prowess. They were chopping wood, growing food, nursing babies - whatever it took to build a life - with that confidence that physically strong people exude. My mother was a Carnegie, a grand name for a not-so-grand family. Her ancestry was vague but had traces of the theatrical, the bohemian and possibly the alcoholic. The few family photos she had showed family members smiling at gatherings in nondescript houses.

*****

It amazed me how quickly the years passed and Jackie and I were ready to leave home. She left and carved out a life in England. She said she wanted a change and wanted to travel. I stayed in a quiet corner of Sydney eking out a life as a writer. Odd really, Jackie the physical one over there in the cold close to all that culture and history and me, the bookworm in the hot, outdoor, beach culture of Sydney.

After five years away Jackie rang me out of the blue. She was back for a week and could she stay with me? I spruced up my rented flat and hid all my work in progress files but I knew whatever I did, it wouldn't be her sort of place. "Where did you get these? Darling no-one uses spice racks anymore." She complained about the vegetarian meals and the heat but somehow we seemed to get on in an odd sort of way. She asked me how my writing was going but, to my relief, never asked to read any.

She showed me photos of her travels and her passion for hang gliding. She talked about the rush and the thrill and the feeling of freedom. She was proud that the flexible ski wing design that was in general use now was designed by a guy from Grafton. She told me about thermals and ridge lift and convergence, using air currents to rise and glide for hours on end. Her voice trailed into the background and the second chapter of my novel took its place. She sensed I wasn't listening. "Laura, Laura." Her raised voice cut through my thoughts. "Funny isn't it? Me hang gliding and you…is that why you don't travel Laura, is it the height thing and planes, is that it?"

"I don't think so. I have flown."

"What to Brisbane?" She laughed.

"Does it matter how far?"

"Course."

"I don't see what that's got to do with it. I don't want to continue with this Ok." She agreed and we carried on looking at her hang gliding shots. To relieve her agitation at the slow pace of my life we decided to have a day in the Blue Mountains. Do some bush walking - it would be good for me to get outside and I knew she'd be up for it.

*****

It was the height of summer and the river at the bottom of the gully was low - we hadn't had rain for months. The warm, thick air simmered, releasing traces of eucalypt vapour. After following the bush path for about ten minutes we found a flat sandstone area. In the distance were the eucalyptus covered escarpments.

"It's the released oil that makes the blue." I commented.

"I know." Jackie replied.

My sandwiches were a disaster. They had worked their way to the bottom of my backpack and become molded around my drink bottle. The compressed bread felt like damp clay and the pickles had oozed out onto the cling wrap. "Sandwiches aren't really the best thing for backpacking are they?" Said Jackie. What she meant was I'd made a dumb decision to make sandwiches. I should have packed crackers, dried fruit and carrot sticks.

We tried to nibble a bit of sandwich then we walked back. Jackie spoke. "Remember that day we had sandwiches in the cubby I'd built for you." She paused.

"What was really going on with you that day?" I felt my face reddening after all those years. "What made you think of that?" I said.

"Dunno, just walking in the bush I suppose. Just got a sudden flash of that scene."

"I don't remember it clearly." I lied.

"Oh yes you do Laura. Come on. God you're difficult, always so closed." I didn't answer and she left it at that.

*****

About half way back to the car she stopped and said she wanted a photo. She wanted to show her friends in London what the Aussie bush really looked like. I found a beautiful gnarled banksia still in flower and pretended to look casual leaning up against a branch close to one of the honey colored flower spikes.

After adjusting her new camera and taking several shots she told me to look more cheerful. "My friends'll think you don't like me being here." She laughed.

"God, you must have hated me. Always ordering you around and getting you to do things with me." She laughed again. We walked on and she noticed a sign to a lookout just off the path. She left me and ran into the bush. The lookout was one of those wooden platforms clinging to the edge of the escarpment. She was leaning over the iron railings.

"Not quite your scene sis. Two hundred metres I'd say." I walked towards her to join her. "Don't Laura it's too high, you'll get nervous." Her voice was high and tense. I walked confidently onto the wooden platform and leaned as far as I could over the railing.

"Three hundred more like." I shouted then lifted my head and laughed. Her face was tight and her mouth was set so hard her lips looked false.

"You lied that day in the cubby. About being scared of heights. You lied to me."

"Of course." I replied, still laughing. She turned and walked away.

We didn't speak the whole way back and very little that night. The incident was never mentioned again. She left the next day having said as little as possible in the fifteen hours it took her to leave. The following week I received a polite note from Jackie with a book about Shakespeare. She sent me the photos she'd taken that day. I never dreamt I'd never see her again.

*****

After hearing about Jackie's accident I was in a haze of grief and exhaustion. Mum and Dad came to stay and gave me copies of lots of old photos of Jackie and me playing. Her exuberant energy was so clearly captured in contrast to me - usually sitting or looking on from a distance. They were very tired the whole time and didn't really want to do much. They said grief was the most exhausting thing they'd ever gone through. But there was one place they did want to go and that was to where Jackie had taken that last photo of me in front of the old Banksia. We packed our bush walking gear and headed for the Grosse Valley.

Up on the escarpment I remembered the exact path as we walked deeper into the bush. We came to the place where I'd told Jackie about the gum vapour. A little way on I found the Banksia. It looked the same with its brush-like blossoms and its spiky leaves. I showed my parents how I had posed and where she had stood to take the photo. Mum insisted on taking a branch with a flower head on it.

They'd planned to stay for a week but they left early. I think they'd done what they came to do. At the airport Mum held me tight for a long time as if she was afraid to let me go. She then held both my hands in hers and told me that the one consolation to her was that Jackie had died hang-gliding - doing the thing she loved most. She said she understood why I hadn't been able to come to the funeral with that long haul flight to the UK. Then she added how ironic she thought it was that Jackie'd died doing hang gliding when I was afraid of heights and that she couldn't believe we were so different. She hugged me once again and told me to keep working hard at my writing.

Linda Robson Bell

Linda Robson Bell was born in the decade after World War II into an extended family whose roots can be traced back to very early settlers in Britain. Many of Linda's relatives still inhabit this cold, beautiful, wild part of northeast England while Linda now lives in the sunny southern hemisphere city of Sydney.

Always an avid reader and scribbler, after two decades as a professional social worker Linda started writing seriously during mid life and this led her to complete a Master of Arts in Creative Writing at the University of Sydney.

Linda's draws from her love of both England and Australia, her exposure to all manner of human behaviour during her social work years, magic, mystery and her lifelong and ever deepening interest in life and spirituality.

After finishing her creative writing studies Linda penned short stories while creating and teaching writing courses including 4-day residential retreat courses in Personal Writing for the Quest for Life Foundation.

Linda is excited to be currently completing her first novel and a book about writing.

Linda loves to hear from people about their writing and life. She runs The Wellspring Centre with programs for writers, coaches and counsellors and a gathering of, writings, books and resources for those of us who write, read and ponder on life's mysterious and wondrous ways.

Thank You for reading
Bittersweet Short Stories

As a writer I really appreciate you supporting my work and as my way of saying *Thank You* I want to give you a complete copy of my ebook:

'A Story to Tell'
a practical guide to writing your autobiography

Just go to: www.astorytotellbook.com

Leave your name and email address and I'll send you a complete copy of 'A Story to Tell' - which will guide you through the whole process of writing your autobiography or memoir.

'A Story to Tell' has over 80 pages and includes:
- a complete framework to structure your autobiography,
- exercises to help you recall memories and turn them into stories
- creative techniques to deepen and improve your writing skills

Visit Linda's sites at:
www.thewellspringcentre.com
www.astorytotellbook.com
or write to Linda at: info@thewellspringcentre.com